Deadly Shorts

Is A Forest Green Original Product

And A Small Potato Production©2020

ISBN 9781989887042-2

DEADLY SHORTS

A COLLECTION OF SHORT STORIES
By Alex McLellan

DEATH CAN'T BE ALL BAD

This book is dedicated to my loving
husband, Ken McLellan .

Without his love, support, and creativity,
my life-long publishing dreams

would have never come to pass.

Ironic.. A love like ours and yet I
struggle to find the words.

I love you madly.

Author's Notes

One of the best aspects about writing is the ability to tell stories in many different styles. This collection embraces that ability.

That being said, the theme of death runs rampantly throughout this book, but reading one story will not prepare you for the next one and this is done with purpose and intention.

After all, death can't be all bad!

Contents

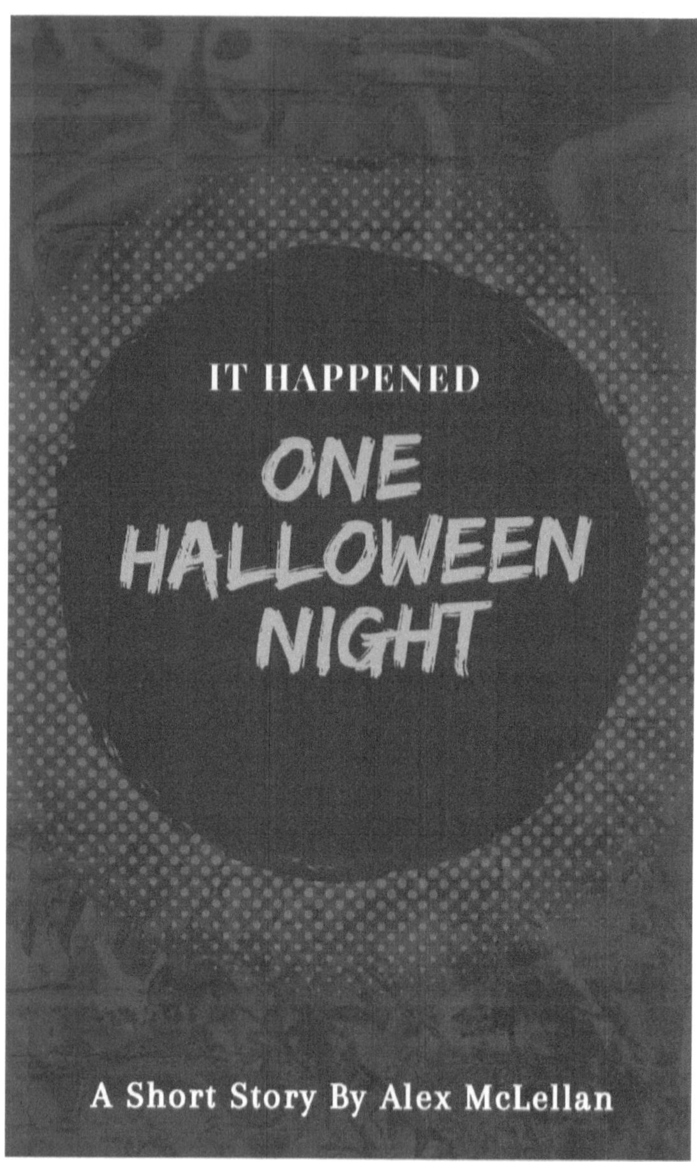

IT HAPPENED
ONE HALLOWEEN NIGHT
A Short Story By Alex McLellan

It Happened One Halloween Night

It was cold this year. People began preparing for winter while still in September. This October Halloween evening was just like every other. Costumed children scurried here and there, occasionally tripping on their heavy garments. Parents walked along the sidewalks patrolling and watching for children's safety.

Mr. Crothers was comfortably never more than eight feet away from his children. He was only a couple of blocks from his house. This was his neighbourhood, and as with the other neighbours, a certain comfort found in familiarity seemed to permeate the festivities and encouraged excitement. However, he was thinking that this particular house would probably be the last to allow the children to visit because of the cold.

It could have happened to any parent, but this night, Mr. Crothers made the mistake of turning his head for just a moment while his children marched up the walkway to the house. When he glanced back, his three and five year old were gone.

In the chilled night air, he found himself frantically searching everywhere. Panic stricken, he found a little Tigger the cat, but once unmasked, was left embarrassed and broken-hearted. Mr. Crothers' children were missing…

Hours passed like moments while the next second seemed to last an eternity as Mr. Crothers' emotional roller coaster made him nauseous with a pounding headache that would not let up. Excruciating was the only way to describe the torment of the anxious, gut-wrenching fear and waiting.

Police, newspapers, television, neighbours, endless searching day in and day out produced nothing. There wasn't a single clue to the children's whereabouts. Mr. Crothers visited the police station each morning and stayed there until very late each night. He hadn't slept in the three days since the children had disappeared.

Mrs. Crothers unable to cope, was placed on sedatives, but even in her medically induced state, tears streamed down her cheeks uncontrollably. On the fourth day, a beautiful, bright sunny day, an exhausted Crothers pulled out of his driveway and headed towards the police station.

Perhaps being exhausted, Crothers' mind opened to possibilities, and that was when he passed the last house he had been with the kids on that fateful Halloween night.

"Trees on the front lawn," he thought to himself, "Already wrapped in burlap," a bitter reminder that his children were lost in the cold.

Crothers drove slowly becoming increasingly fixated on the trees he had just noticed and unable to release his focus, he continued staring into his rear view mirror, scrutinizing the trees as something caught his attention. A tiny orange piece of something flickered in the wind near the base of one of the trees.

He immediately spun the car into reverse. Suddenly his heart quickened and a wave of certainty came over him. He pulled over and with the car still running, leaving the driver's door wide open, he ran to the trees now certain they had not been there on Halloween night. The small orange piece of something seemed to be calling to him. Could this be the tail of his daughter's Halloween costume? Could he afford not to check? Feeling slightly foolish, he tugged the plastic and began unwrapping the burlap.

Badly bruised, still bleeding, his daughter's almost lifeless body fell to the ground. Alive! She was alive! He held his daughter in his arms and his short lived gratitude was overcome with a sickening foreshadowing feeling as he reached out to the next tree and poked it with his finger. No movement.

Crothers, crying, having fallen to his knees, scooping his daughter in his arms, kissing her forehead, he turned and shouted towards the house, "You bastard!"

He looked back to the little burlap figure then gently placed his daughter on the ground. He cautiously pulled away the burlap, struggling to conquer the sickening feeling of dread. He very carefully removed his son from the lawn stake to which he had been tied and bound. He placed the boy beside his sister on the lawn, staring so intently, almost willing the boy to life, and to his shock, the boy slowly began to open his eyes, "I knew you would find me, Daddy," the boy whispered.

In a fleeting moment, life had changed again for the Crothers' family and after some healing and time would pass, even more changes would reveal themselves.

The house where the children had gone missing was owned by a recluse in his early thirties. It was rumoured he was a very simple person being the only survivor of a car accident that killed both his parents. He was a quiet, unassuming man, pleasant, didn't speak much, would sometimes wave to those who passed by, and he was always tending his garden.

Yes, in the days that followed other burlap covered trees found on the property were examined by authorities. Yes, beneath the burlap, more missing children, some from as far away as across state lines and yes, found dead, ten in all.

It has been said that once a person's mind opens and sees what is right in front of them, the mind's door cannot be closed and a person will always see what is hiding in plain sight. Whether that is true or not, one thing is absolutely certain for those exposed to this particular Halloween incident, when a neighbourhood betrayed by one of its own were shocked to their core, forever relieving them of complete trust. This was especially true for Mr. Crothers and his neighbours. These people were affected. These people would discover an unavoidable, overwhelming draw to burlap covered trees for the rest of their lives, many so compelled, they found themselves walking into a neighbour's yard or stranger's yard, gently kicking the burlap covered tree, just to err on the side of caution.

The End

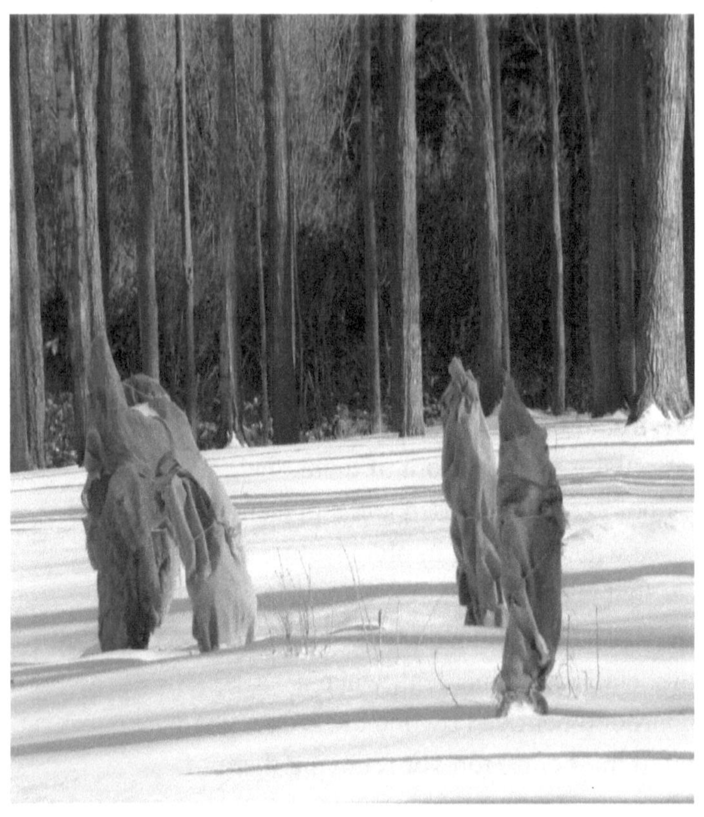

"The above photo was taken on a property located on a busy highway on the outskirts of Shelburne, Ontario. Thousands have driven by this property. This image will haunt me for the rest of my life because my mind was open and I…never checked."   Alex McLellan

The Mourning Window

A Short Story By Alex McLellan

The Mourning Window

I distinctly remember when I first returned home, really returned home. The gripping sense of long awaited familiarity was almost overwhelming. The trees, cracks in the sidewalk, the creepy sound of the fence swaying back and forth in the wind, the smell of baking, Downey scent from the dryer, and the laughter. The laughter came from the kids playing street hockey. I used to be one of those kids, we both were, me and my brother Nathan.

I began to remember how I raced Nathan to the old church. I always won the race. I'd rush up to the bell tower window and watch him staggering behind, laughing his fool heart out. I remember his laughter so vividly, so infectious, I would giggle as I watched.

He'd run up the hill, up the stairs, giggling and stumbling, and he would call to me, "I'm saving it just for you, David!"

I could hear him, foot heavy on the top few stairs. I would be hiding in the usual spot.

"It's a big one! I'm gonna find you and when I do, boy!"

Of course as our ritual would have it, he'd find me. He would lean over, bum towards me, and fart. He'd fart the biggest, loudest, smelly fart he could muster! This was how Nathan explained never winning the race.

"I can't run fast while I'm saving farts!" I can still hear him giggling, red faced, out of breath from running.

Like yesterday, his scream rips through my heart as it sounds so clearly in my mind.

"I got you!" he had gloated only moments before.

The snapping of wood, brittle and dry, bearing promise of foreshadowing as the old floor gave way.

"Nathan !" I screamed at the inevitable as I helplessly watched. He lay broken, awkward, a smiling ragdoll, fifty feet below, smiling and dead. My brother was dead! Over and over again I said these words to myself but it would never become real to me.

I remember not having to go to the funeral. Instead, I raced to the church even though I was banned from the building. I ran pretending Nathan was just behind, and he was…They carried him to his lifeless, cold, little grave as I watched from the church. I now watched from the mourning window.

Thirty-five years later, and still, whenever I visited my mother, I'd always race to the church. Year after year, I searched for Nathan to appear on the other side of that damn window. A rational man, yet I truly longed and secretly hoped by some miracle this would happen.

Upon one of our visits, while I searched relentlessly out the mourning window, I watched my son run up the hill to find me. He was giggling and stumbling.

"I found you!" he shouted up to me.

I smiled deeply moved.

I saw Nathan returned to me through the mourning window I had prayed at for most of my life.

"Dad?" he called to me while I stood in the fantasy of a dear memory.

"Dad!" How I missed my little brother.

"Dad! C'mon! I'll race you back! Give me a head start, o.k.?"

My face lit up.

"Just till I can't see you out the window," I answered in a weakened voice.

"Deal!" he agreed and the giggling began.

I watched my son running down the hill. He stumbled as he turned to me, laughing as he waved.

"Good-bye, Nathan." I whispered in a tearful chopped breath. "I promise to remember you and love you always, little brother."

And I ran after my son for the rest of my life because I loved him dearly. I vowed to teach my son all of life's most important lessons.

Farting was only the beginning…

The End

Some Lady !

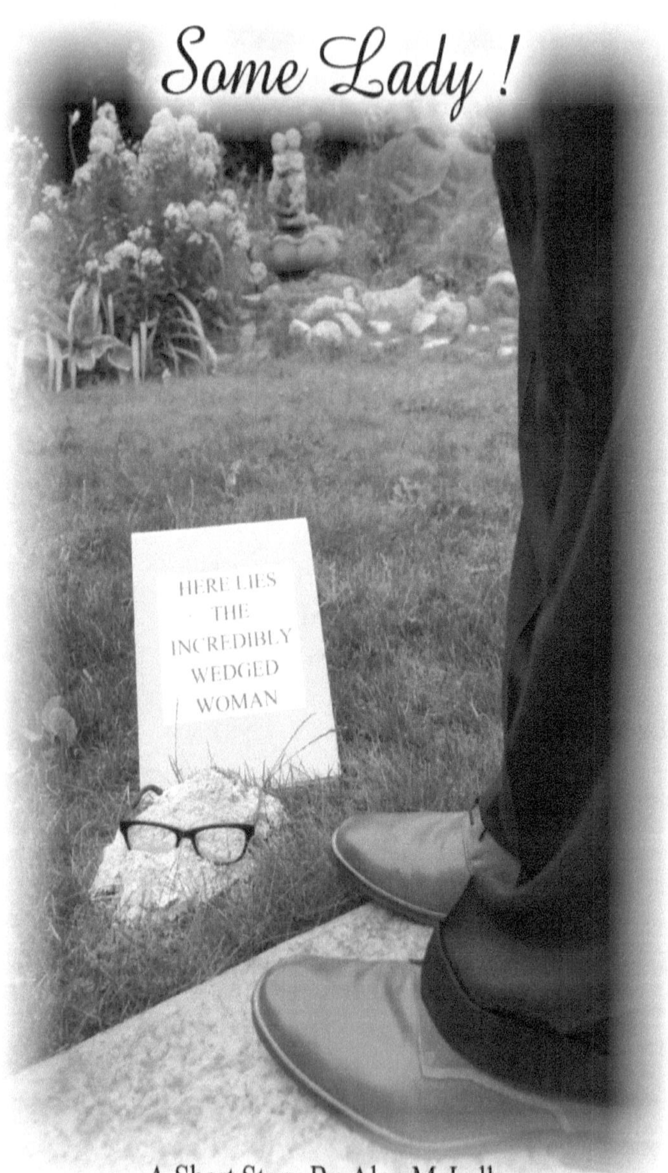

A Short Story By Alex McLellan

Some Lady!

I'm sitting on our roof patio. From here I can see all the people of the city making their way somewhere. The business suits, unemployed, students, seniors, and there's a woman down on the street who has caught my attention. The woman is in her forties, fit looking, and in a hurry. She has on these old librarian type of black framed glasses. I smile as I think how funny she looks and wonder what she'd do if she could see herself the way I do. A thin wire frame would suit her so much better. I miss my mother.

When my mother died a few weeks ago, I had no idea how my life would change. She spent time with me before she died. Even then, all she could do was worry about me and my brother. When I asked her why she was like that, she said it was only obvious now that she worried about us because she was lying around and not keeping busy doing the housework.

We had a lot of fun some of those days before she left. I remember taking her for a walk in the park. It was pretty cold that day and we spent more time dressing her than we did walking. The wheel chair was sometimes awkward on bumps and I remember getting her wheel wedged at one point in the parking lot by the walkway entrance to the park. A large, strong looking young man wearing a suit, just happened to come by and asked, "I couldn't help but notice… Would you like a hand?"

My mother had been slightly grumpy that day and short on patience, understandably so in her condition. She looked up at the man, peering at him over her glasses with an absurd look on her face, "Well actually young man, I'm dying soon, any minute in fact, and would like nothing more than to die here in this parking lot, wedged in this exact spot. You see, I'm hoping to be cremated and with any luck they'll spread my ashes right here. It was no fluke that you and I met. The next time you come this way you might take notice of a small pile of ashes and take a moment of silence in my memory as, "The Incredibly Wedged Woman".

The man stood stunned, eyes wide. I don't think he knew what to say. I don't think he knew if my mother was serious or not. They stared at each other for a few seconds and finally my mother said, "Yes, yes! If you could see your way to help us, me, it would be greatly appreciated." He lifted her out with ease and my mother and I thanked him. As he walked on he seemed to look back at us quite often. His nervousness made my mom chuckle. She had that effect on people. No one knew if and when she was serious.

When I was a child, we were vegetarians and as the years passed I could never make myself enjoy meat. When meat eating relatives came over for dinner they never knew what to expect. On one occasion my grandparents came to dinner. My grandfather, a very out spoken man in his eighties, a meat eater, would always find something negative to comment on with reference to the vegetarian lifestyle. My mother made vegetarian pasta, vegetarian meat balls, garlic bread, and salad. He took one bite of his salad and spat it out almost immediately, suspicious, not understanding that the salad was just salad, not some nefarious vegetarian concoction.

"What the hell kind of food is this? Don't you have any real food? What's in here anyway?"

His reaction gave my mom license to let him have it and she let him have it!

"Well Dad, I debated about what to make for you."

"Finally the God-Damned truth comes out. Let's hear it!"

"First I had my son bring me three frogs, then I added a few loose eye-balls I had around the house and I boiled them together. I rinsed them off, then they were finely chopped and mixed with onion. Ah, but when I remembered you were coming I substituted bone fragments I was saving from my knee operation instead of croutons. You may be wondering what I made the fake meat balls with… Let's just say, have you seen that little furry scrap you call a dog lately?"

He stared at her for a long time with his lips pressed together, harboring a disgusted look on his face. Everyone at the table was silent. My Dad put his face in his hands and he pressed his lips together trying not to laugh. Grandpa turned to my

Grandmother and said, "Did you bring those extra batteries? I can't hear a damn thing!"

Even though we all knew mom wasn't serious, we were more comfortable eating the meatballs after Buffy the dog sauntered into the room. Then did we laugh!

"What the hell is so God-Damned funny? None of you have ever seen a dog before? You vegetarians! At least you got the meatballs right! Thank you for that much!" Grandpa sounded off in disapproval enjoying his veggie meatballs. Everyone was giddy and giggling. My grandmother just shook her head. Grandpa was such a character. He may well be where mom got her spunk from. My mother caught my Dad's eye and winked with that bratty smirk of hers. Dad loved my mother's off beat sense of humour and being best friends, he knew something like this was going to happen. People at his office always looked forward to the retelling of our family dinners. Now, when I think back, what great memories we shared.

My mother wrote articles, short stories, made greeting cards, created crafts, woodwork, baked dog biscuits, painted, cartooned, and dabbled in advertising. She was a visual merchandiser, and entrepreneur. She was physically fit and had over twelve years' experience in the health food industry. She often said she was still a statistic because she was white, married with two children, with no education. Sometimes this would irritate her. She told me once how successful you are depends on so many factors, it's much easier to just be happy, and work hard. Measure success by the goals you set for yourself and see which ones you achieve just trying your best. Once you get there you take a step back and see if you're still happy or miserable. She also said that nothing is impossible, not really. Skill can be achieved, knowledge can be acquired, and life takes time. Faith in life never hurts. It's always good to smile. A person does not have to have the same profession their whole life. Honesty is almost always the best policy and it's very important to earn another day. She believed doing good deeds raised a person's spirit. She was also very fond of laughing and she always offered very good advice.

I suppose it goes without saying that my dad is pretty much devastated but he tries hard to carry on. He said he will not disgrace her memory by choosing not to live each day as she would have wanted, but he is really missing her and all her antics.

Mom set money aside for my brother to travel before she died. He never asked for it but it was just something she knew he wanted and needed to do. She also knew he was stingy and a work horse. She set it up in her will that he was to receive an annual travel expense for a major trip each year for the next ten years. He could only get the money if he travelled. If he didn't relax traveling once a year, the money would be donated to the Hair Replacement For Men Company. So even if he didn't want to take time off, it was better than living with where all that hard earned money had gone, and he'd never let that happen. Mom always said things like, "Well, it's your decision. I'd never tell you what to do." That's where he is now, of course "he decided" to travel. The Bahamas are just what he needed to help deal with his loss. Mom knew he would have returned to work and never taken time to heal. She was wise.

With me she took a different approach. I couldn't decide what I wanted to do with my life. I'd hang out at my Mom's store, helping customers, filling orders, creating, but it wasn't me. Mom spent fifteen years building that business. It was so quaint, a café, book store, craft store, a community hub where people performed in the evenings. One day when we were there together she mentioned she'd like to paint the place. I agreed.

"You don't like this color anymore?" she asked.

"What do you mean?" I answered.

"Well, you picked it out. You picked out the lights. You chose the tables."

"I did!?"

"Oh troubled youth, lest we forget. I'll think about it some more."

Before she died she gave the business to me. She told me to make it my own. After she reminded me how much a part of it I already was, I loved the idea. It was what I wanted to do all along, my own business. She told me that I'd tried other things, achieved them, still wasn't happy. Working in the store was what made me happy. She said never to be afraid to keep on trying. If in a few years, I changed my mind, then that's what will happen. In her own words, "Just be happy, honey. There is a little something you could do for me in return."

She looked at me pleadingly with those ugly librarian glasses at the tip of her nose. She realized I was looking at those glasses. "Beauty is in the eye of the beholder and while you're looking at me, I'm looking at you! C'mon honey, let's have some fun. Don't tell your father. He wouldn't approve. Tell your brother."

Ah, but I will tell my father because I know it will cheer him up.

That brings me to what I'm doing here today. My mother enjoyed studying human nature. I still can't believe I'm doing this.

I'm on our roof patio across from the park. Oh, there he is, my mother's victim. I better hurry. I'm following mom's instructions to the letter. I'm dressed as an old woman. I've got the cane, powdered wig and everything.

I rushed to the park bench at the parking lot where Mom and I got the wheel chair stuck on that cold day. I took a small mountain of ashes from the fireplace and poured them out there in 'the spot' and I placed a little sign on a lawn spike which reads, 'HERE LIES THE INCREDIBLY WEDGED WOMAN'.

Mom and I had seen the man frequently walking that way and I was instructed to wait today. He walked briskly up to me and passed me and then happened to notice the sign. He took a step back and read the sign again. He sighed, deeply moved and pulled a tissue out of his pocket. He took a moment of silence and wiped his eyes. That was my cue.

"Did you know her, sonny?" I asked in my best old lady voice.

"Nah, she was just some lady." He walked away snivelling.

"You don't know the half of it. She really was Some Lady!" I said to myself laughing as I walked away. I just bet she's still around somewhere, wearing those dumb glasses, laughing and laughing. I really enjoyed doing this. Mom could always get me to reach outside my comfort zone. I missed my mother dearly.

I put my hand in the overcoat pocket and felt paper.

"What's this?" I asked myself. I could feel the tears welling up.

"You didn't think you'd get off that easy, did you? Hope you enjoyed the incredibly wedged woman. I knew you'd keep your promise and then you would find my note. When you get bored or need some excitement, I'm always here to help. I love you, honey."

It was a note written by my mother which included a long list of tasks for me to do when I was ready. The tasks were outrageous! At the very bottom, she had drawn a little picture of those funny librarian glasses and beside it she wrote, "C'mon honey, let's have some fun!" I could see her in my mind's eye with that bratty smirk, "Thanks mom," I whispered.

The End

THE DOCTOR
A SHORT STORY BY
ALEX MCLELLAN

The Doctor

Once upon a time there was a person who believed within his very soul, rested the most incredible story. He wasn't absolutely certain what that story might be, but he was very self-assured the story was great, beyond expectation. He entered an online writing contest hosted by a virtual stranger.

The person who owned these thoughts was a doctor, an actual country-visit-you-at-home-doctor, a much needed and respected man in his small community. But in quiet moments when the office was vacant of patients and no one was dying or in need, the doctor, a well-travelled man, travelled to a place where he had never travelled before. Inside his imaginary reverie lay an imaginary utopia where people only suffered colds and the likes, nothing life threatening, nothing detrimental.

And in this imaginary place, in the heart of his soul, he often remembered a young man, a patient who had killed himself. The doctor struggled with this particular patient's passing as he believed himself to be the bringer of good health, the keeper of patient's truths, and always felt he had failed the young man.

Even through this self-perceived guilt via failure, the doctor's imagination did not falter, and a culmination of all he knew and everywhere he had ever been became his new utopia, his sanctuary, his peace of mind, literal piece of mind, and in writing this story, his story, found himself a keystroke away from genius, finally.

The virtual stranger, the one responsible for the contest, was no stranger to writing, a savant, an intellect, a cerebral challenge to all who aspired to be great.

He watched on virtually and awaited his response to the challenge. The story must begin with, "Once upon a time", and end with, "they lived happily ever after."

The inventor of the challenge was quite eager to see and read and feel something the equivalent to his own inspirational moving moment, when spirit visits and creates genius. All those who accepted the challenge knew it was an uphill battle, except for the doctor. After all, they had only virtually met. The doctor simply had something to share and he did so in the only way he knew how. The doctor had no hope or inclination of winning a contest at this point as his goal was simply to be read.

And so he began with what he knew, and he hoped by the end of his tale, he would find peace nestled deeply within his well-established imaginary utopia.

'Once upon a time there was a young man who visited his family doctor begging for help to stop the voices in his head. The doctor compassionately began a course of treatment and the young man seemed to be revelling in his new found relief. As time went on, the doctor came to realise there were many different personalities within this young man's mind and the treatment would have to be modified. The doctor struggled to help this young man and sought the help of many advisors. As more time passed, the young man seemed to be responding to the doctor's treatment. He recalled the last visit they had together.

"How are you today, Derrick?"

"Oh, a little groggy, but things are quiet today, thankfully. I've noticed I'm a little tired and I can't remember some things. I lost an hour today," Derrick answered in a sad, exhausted voice.

As if a light switched on in the young man's eyes, a second personality surfaced.

"Well hello there, Doc! Long-time no see. Whaaaat's up?" Ty was a very abrasive personality.

"Ty, yes it's been a long time."

"Still trying to kill me? It'll never happen!"

"Derrick doesn't want this anymore. He's tired. He wants to be himself all the time, Ty. You need to leave," the doctor encouraged.

"No fuck'n way! If anyone is go'n anywhere, it's that pussy!"

Personality number three could not contain himself.

"I apologize for his rudeness, doctor. I mean, present thyself with some sense of decorum! But truly, I didn't intentionally overhear, it is difficult for me not to eavesdrop from time to time. No one tells us anything, you know."

"Hello Winston."

"I have an important question. What will happen to the likes of Derrick and myself if that wretched creature Ty manages to take over?"

"Hopefully that won't happen."

"But if it does?"

"I will do my best to take care of Derrick, Winston. Derrick's welfare must come first. I am trying to stress that to all of you."
"All of us? How many of us are there?" Winston was truly concerned.

"You don't know?" the doctor asked.

"No, I most certainly do not! When I arrived I was under the impression there were only three occupants to this building!" Winston's anger surfaced.

Suddenly as if being rescued mentally, somehow Derrick managed to find his way back.

"Welcome back."

"Not again," Derrick responded in disappointment.

"Yes, I'm afraid so."

"Am I going to be ok? I am so tired. I don't remember being this tired ever before."

"That's enough for today, Derrick. Have you given any thought to my proposal and the possibility of you entering the hospital full time for a while?"

"Yah, but I was scared until today. I don't know what happened, but I've never been this tired."

"Great news, Derrick. At the hospital we can keep you safe and I'll be able to visit three to five times a week instead of just once a week like we do now."

"Alright. Let's do it."

And with that, Derrick found himself at the hospital where the doctor hoped his patient could find rest.

It wasn't until two day days later the doctor was awoken at 4 a.m. and received the news of Derrick's suicide. The doctor's heart sank with guilt. Eventually the doctor was able to read the young man's suicide note.

"There once was a convict named Ty who roomed with a dick of a guy.

And after a spell, though difficult to tell, he killed Derrick, that dick of guy.

He killed the God Damned Brit, Winston, the git, and when all was said and done,

He went to finish the doctor. There could only be one."

This was the peace the Doctor had sought. He smiled to himself. Now he could live out his days with the last remaining personality, Emily, whom the Doctor believed Ty had never been conscious of. With Ty completely medicated never to surface again, only one question remained. Would the Doctor win the contest and live happily ever after? The End.'

The Doctor remembered the satisfaction he experienced pressing the send button on the computer and it wasn't until that moment, he had considered the possibility he may win the contest.

The doctor walked over to the locked door and shouted down the hall, "Hey is the mail here yet?"

An orderly shouted back, "Nope! Not yet, Doc."

It didn't matter, not really, it was just a formality, a matter of curiosity.

"Let me know when it comes, I'm waiting on the results of a writing contest!"

The orderly turned to the floor nurse who asked, "Contest?"

The orderly shook his head. "No m'am. No contest, no doctor, just some poor bastard and whoever else is knocking around in that attic of his. He's more than a few sandwiches short of a picnic basket, if yah get my meaning?"

Ah but alas what did any of it matter as long as the doctor remained with his beloved Emily and we can't forget the genius new friend and literary challenger.

"I'm pleased to meet you. Pardon me? What was that? Well of course I lived happily ever after!

After all, Emily and Ty are murderers, not me!"

The End

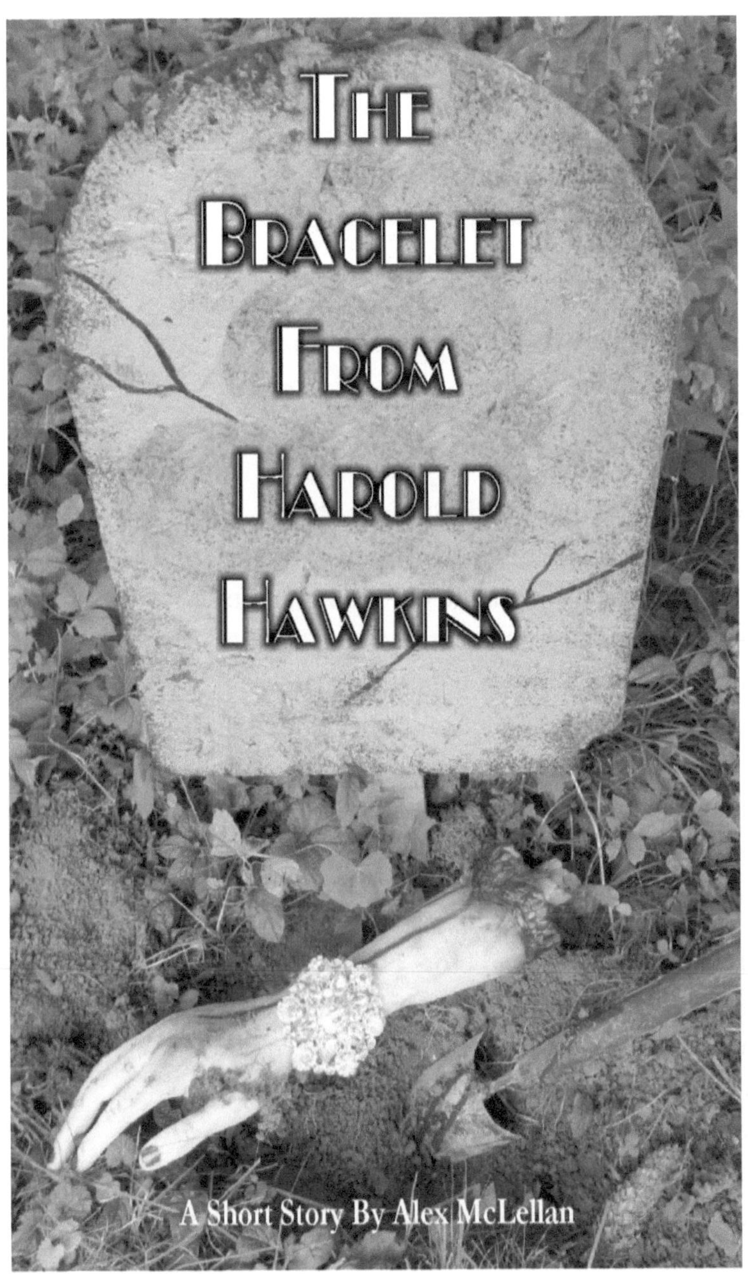
The Bracelet From Harold Hawkins
A Short Story By Alex McLellan

The Bracelet From Harold Hawkins

I don't remember much about middle school, but I remember Willard. He had long dark brown greasy hair, wore baggy black t-shirts, baggy second hand jeans that were frayed at the bottoms as they rested on his older brother's hand-me-down All Star runners. He looked dishevelled and uncared for. No one ever took Willard the Weird seriously, after all, his name really was 'Willard,' not Bill or William. He was always doing things that were so strange to us. He would walk around mumbling to himself as he read aloud from a comic book, and he always carried a brown paper bag that was grease stained and soiled. We never cared enough to ever ask him what was in it. We always laughed at him. What else could we do? We didn't know any better, kids can be so mean.

I remember once, just before Halloween in grade seven, we had to tell ghost stories that we made up. There were the usual stories of gore and appendages who were possessed by evil demons until eventually, towards the last few people, Willard amongst, we sat bored out of our minds convinced nothing could ever faze us.

Poor Victoria was busy telling her very boring and not frightening tale of the ghost of the killer poodle, when she stopped short. Feeling ill at the stress of public speaking, she ran from the room at high speed to visit the bathroom. Then came Willard and unbeknownst to us then, twenty-five of us were about to be fazed.

Willard carried a guitar case wrapped in a black plastic bag. Something reeked as he made his way to the front of the class. This did not faze us, convincingly disgusting, but there was more. Miss Spencer politely covered her nose as Willard wrapped a bandanna around the front of his face, cowboy style.

"For the last two weeks," began Willard the Weird, in his best attempt at achieving his version of a 'cool' tone of voice. "We have endured the most boring and dumb stories about Halloween. I mean, give me a break, killer poodles from hell?"

We laughed with our peer at poor Victoria's expense. It was good her head was busy throwing up. Her feelings would have been hurt.

Willard continued. "So, on this very special Halloween, I decided to involve you all in a true life Halloween experience. You will thank and remember me for years to come. Proof rests soundly in this case for your entertainment!"

Now, our attention was peeked. Eyes wide, we listened to our otherwise introverted classmate.

"Last Friday evening when the moon was full, I went out on a mission. I placed a stake in my backpack, a large hammer, holy water, a large cross and a mirror. I went in search of vampires." We howled, with no pun intended. This was going to be another stupid, boring, Halloween story!

"I walked around for two hours until I thought to myself, 'Willard, my boy,'"

By this time, Miss Spencer was becoming uncomfortable with the smell of the PROOF, and moved to the back of the classroom coughing occasionally.

"What you really need to do is to look at the situation closely. Vampires, ghosts and goblins probably hang out near the graveyard, hmm..." Willard tapped his finger several times at his chin cupping his hand on his face.

Once again, he caught our curiosity as he paced back and forth in front of the blackboard. "So that's what I did. I went to the graveyard. It was kind' a foggy, and you know what? You hear the strangest sounds. I love that place, man! Anyway, it started to get cold and soon it would be morning and I was really disappointed that I didn't run into any vampires especially, so I went home."

"Good ending, Willard!" Came heckling from the back of the classroom amongst booing and jeering.

"So of course, I went back again. I was convinced I'd find something of interest to share with such fond peers of mine."

Victoria always wore the same hard heeled shoes, and we could hear she was very slowly making her way back to us. Willard continued.

"So I searched and searched, but nothing…then I finally remembered old Mrs. Hawkins passed on three weeks ago. Remember her? Remember how tiny and feeble she was?"

We were curious and Victoria's footsteps made the suspense and anticipation grow.

"I walked around a little bit until I came to her grave. It was real good fortune I thought to bring a shovel this time I went out. It took me, oh about half an hour of digging until I hit the

coffin. What a glorious sound! That shovel–
'ting' sound, like I struck gold or something."

He slowly began un-wrapping the proof as we
could hear Victoria would make her entrance
any moment and the class was riveted. In the
silence Willard triumphantly proclaimed, "I
opened the coffin and everything! But let me tell
you, she didn't look her best! I didn't think any
of you would believe me so I cut off her arm to
show you!"

And he had done this thing! Like a proud
hunter, he held the decaying arm of old Mrs.
Hawkins up high above his head for all to view.

Poor Victoria entered the room, took one look at
the arm dripping blood and maggots onto the
floor and fainted. Miss Spencer needed more
convincing before she would faint. She slowly
walked to the front of the class and peered at the
arm Willard held.

"Look, Miss Spencer, look!" I was very careful
not to disturb anything important like evidence."
He pointed to the bracelet the whole community
knew was a cherished gift given to Mrs.
Hawkins by her beloved husband, Harold.

Miss Spencer leaned in squinting, focussing on
the bracelet. Well, that was all the convincing

Miss Spencer needed. As she fainted, she whispered to Willard asking, "Willard, how could you?"

This made Willard the Weird blush with true confession and pride.

"O.k." he admitted, "I forgot to bring a knife or saw so I just banged it off with the shovel. Big deal?!" Willard was disappointed to give up his secret. "She didn't need it! Anyhow, she has another one and she doesn't need that one either!" He chuckled sincerely believing he had said something humorous.

THIS COMPLETLEY FAZED US!

Lisa vomited from the ordeal and odour and she did this on Bobby, who then fainted from being vomited on and probably from everything in general. Anthony began laughing in hysterics, some of us just stared straight ahead with our mouths and eyes wide open in shock, and the rest of us had our hands over our noses just trying to mentally process how someone, anyone, could have done this thing Willard had done.

Willard stood at the front of the class asking, "What? What?" still holding the arm forward, not understanding our reaction as he seemed to be waiting for applause and cheers.

Vince raised himself with logic, hopped over the two fainted bodies and summoned the principal, who seemed to run to us at the speed of light.

The Principal, seeing Willard asked, "Willard, what's happening here, young man?"

Willard shrugged his shoulders innocently. "I dunn'o! I was just telling my Halloween story and everyone started puking and fainting and stuff."

The Principal, standing with arms folded squinted and leaned in to examine the proof and seeing the bracelet slowly asked, "Willard, is that the bracelet from Har...What have you done?!"

Those of us still standing, stood still in anticipation as Willard leaned to us and said, "Gotcha Losers! Sheesh! And you call me weird!"

Like a rampage of animals, we jumped over desk tops like a pack of mad dogs in a fury and we ran fast as our legs would carry us toward the graveyard at the end of the street. The Principal followed behind.

There we stood catching our breath as we looked on the extremely undisturbed graves of Mr. and Mrs. Hawkins. The hysterical laughter and giggles followed us back to the school. Even the Principal chuckled, shaking his head.

Willard really did give us something to remember for the rest of our lives. After that day we still called him Willard the Weird, and Willard, well, he preferred it that way.

The End.

"Just For The Hell Of It !"

A Short Story By Alex McLellan

Just For The Hell Of It

To this day, I do not know whether the old woman was daft, insane, lonely, or the most convincing person I've ever met.

Perhaps being old now myself provides me with the time to ponder experiences from my childhood and see how they measure up. Certainly I am wiser now, but a believer in ghosts? Perhaps it's safer to err on the side of caution, who knows?

I first met the old gal at my cousin's boarding house where I usually spent summer vacations as a young girl. Summers were grand! Days of laughter and carefree folly were precious moments shared with a warm breeze and the soothing sounds of the ocean's tides. My Aunt and Uncle tended their boarding house as though they boarded royalty and because of their excellent hospitality, they did quite well for themselves. What a variety of people I was able to meet over my many visits. That was the best part.

When arriving one summer, I immediately saw every familiar site, except for the small, curious looking, old Italian woman. She sat at the end of the balcony and appeared to be speaking to herself and at any time would burst into laughter, hit herself on her lap and say, "Ah, yes! My goodness! Yes! Yes! I remember well!"

My cousin merely shrugged her off as a harmless old woman, a little off her nut, eccentric and a paying customer, but she fascinated me.

Within days my curiosity became the better of me. She sat at the end of the balcony overlooking the ocean. Her dark shawl and black clothing made me think she was a widow from the old country. As the days passed and we spoke, it turned out her husband had died quite young. Unfortunately he died before they had children, one of her regrets she said.

I found her so unique, even if she was a little crazy. Each discussion held new discoveries for me. I found her interesting. Mrs. Brutelli never re-married. Her love for her husband seemed to grow every day, even in his absence.

"Hello."

"Oh, hello Bella," the old woman smiled happily to me. "Lovely day, this day, just'a lovely."

"Well, I reckon, it's too hot," I answered.

"Never you mind, Bella. I drink'a the tea last night and I dreamed about you. You marry and'a have a beautiful baby. Your baby has'a eyes-blue like'a Madonna's gown, you know? Well, you gonna see, Bella. You gonna see."

"I can imagine."

"Happy life for you Bella, happy life."

"I'm glad you think so. I've come to say good-bye. I've enjoyed meeting you."

"Many thanks, Bella. I leave'a soon too, very soon."

I remember as I started walking away, I had to ask, "So who is it you talk to when you are here sitting alone?"

"Oh, I speak'a with my Franko," Mrs. Brutelli smiled lovingly.

"But he's dead. You told me yourself."

"Ah Bella, your mind she is so young. So much to understand."

"But I don't understand."

"His body, he is gone. He lives, Bella, in'a here, and he lives here." And she pointed to her heart and to her temples. "You will know in time, me, I am not crazy. I believe and I still love and Franko lives still. I believe."

We made our farewells and it all seemed to end abruptly, our relationship, my vacation, and the summer.

It makes me wonder though. My husband and I, both brown eyed, had Alla, our beautiful blue eyed daughter. As far as a happy life, the old gal got it very wrong. My husband was a violent drunkard. He's long since gone thankfully and Alla, grown, has children of her own.

Guess its loneliness these days that makes my mind wander with all the time in the world. Seems I always find myself at the boarding house, remembering the ocean and the happy summer days of my youth.

Guess Mrs. Brutelli will always be a part of that. I think I really did feel sorry for the old gal, sitting alone, talking to her poor, dead, Franko. She loved him so fiercely that she believed it was her love that brought him back. She really believed she was talking to him. Ghosts? Foolishness!

Yet, there are moments when I lay in bed, awake, quite alone, almost ready to sleep and I honestly believe I smell alcohol and I swear I hear my dead husband breathing… It can be very upsetting, the very thought of it…

Gives me half a mind to lean over with a pillow and smother him to death a second time, just for the hell of it!

The End

When Mosquitos Bite

A Short Story By Alex McLellan

When Mosquitos Bite

He cautiously gazed at the clock. Twenty-five to
one it diligently reported. In the moonlight he
could see his wife's profile perfectly. His mind
wondered back to a happy ignorant time of life
and love. He remembered when he thought his
wife was the most incredible thing on earth.
How honoured he was to hear her say, "I do"
when they married. Hours upon hours he would
watch her sleep, worried she might stop
breathing.

A mosquito hovered and buzzed around his
head. He blindly swatted without success.
Twenty minutes to one. His anticipation beamed
across his face. He nervously began to perspire.

BUZZ..BUZZ..BUZZ…

"Damn mosquito!" he cursed in a whisper.

TICK,TICK,TICK.. The clock seemed to mock
him somehow.

He looked at his wife carefully now. She looked
so peaceful, asleep on his chest. She looked like
she felt so safe in his arms. He gently moved his
hand across her chest, feeling her almost
shapeless breasts, her now large, wobbly

stomach, her larger and wider than life bum, her rounded shoulders, and her even rounder thighs.

BUZZ…BUZZ…BUZZ…
TICK…TICK…TICK…

Never had time passed so slowly. His heart quickened from the stress. Suddenly it happened again. The anxiety became intolerable.

It was his wife's head that bothered him the most.

"God-Damned mosquito!" he whispered.

He looked at her head as though it were not attached to her body. He saw it now as a separate blob of metabolism that was bleached, foul, loud, wrinkled. It was awful, even unbearable. The very sight of the bleached blob was absolutely repulsive to him. He quickly yanked his arm from beneath the weight of the most sickening thing next to death.

How he hated her.

He hated her screaming, hated her new clothes, her new nail polish, her ear wrenching laugh, the way she now waddled and smoked, and he absolutely detested the clack-stick sound of her dentures. He even hated the smell of her, of her actual body. The air she breathed gnarled his stomach into knots that would ache for hours just imagining the off chance he may have breathed her expressed air, and may have ingested her vileness and disgust.

Yes indeed! He would rejoice to be rid of her. Again he looked over to the clock. His stomach ached with nervous tension and excited anticipation. In only ten minutes he would be a new man. In only eleven minutes, he would have the best sleep in years.

BUZZ…BUZZ…BUZZ..TICK…TICK...TICK

Again he swatted unsuccessfully at the annoying mosquito.

How irritating during what could be and would be the happiest and most satisfying night of his life. His chest began to ache. He perspired and waited and waited and waited.

BUZZ..BUZZ..BUZZ..TICK..TICK ..TICK…

Five, four, three, two….

Suddenly his heart seized. He sat up abruptly. He gasped for breath, for air! He could feel his throat burning in relentless, futile attempts to breathe.

BUZZ…BUZZ…BUZZ...

He fell back onto his pillows, hand upon his chest, unable to move. "But the poison?" he thought. "His wife, she should be.."

TICK…TICK…TICK…

RRRIIINNNGGG! The alarm clock sounded. In his deep pain he could hear that awful voice sarcastically make noise as it formed its question. His wife turned on the light by the bed.

"Having a little heart attack are we?" The female thing he had married so long ago sat up in bed calmly, lit a cigarette, and extended her hand in front of her, examining her nails intently while blowing a puff of smoke across her husband's face.

"I mean, really darling, we could have divorced by you're right. This is far more fun."

His wife had known the whole time. He now approached the moment before death when breathing stops and only consciousness and senses remain. If he could have laughed, he would have. Through the smoke that mockingly floated by him he could hear her ear wrenching voice laugh. She had been awake the whole evening.

BUZZ…BUZZ…BUZZ…

He could see the mosquito as it landed on his forehead.

BUZZ…BUZZ..

"Oh, here darling, let me get that for you."

BUZZ…bite…splat…silence.

The End

In Light Of Ardith

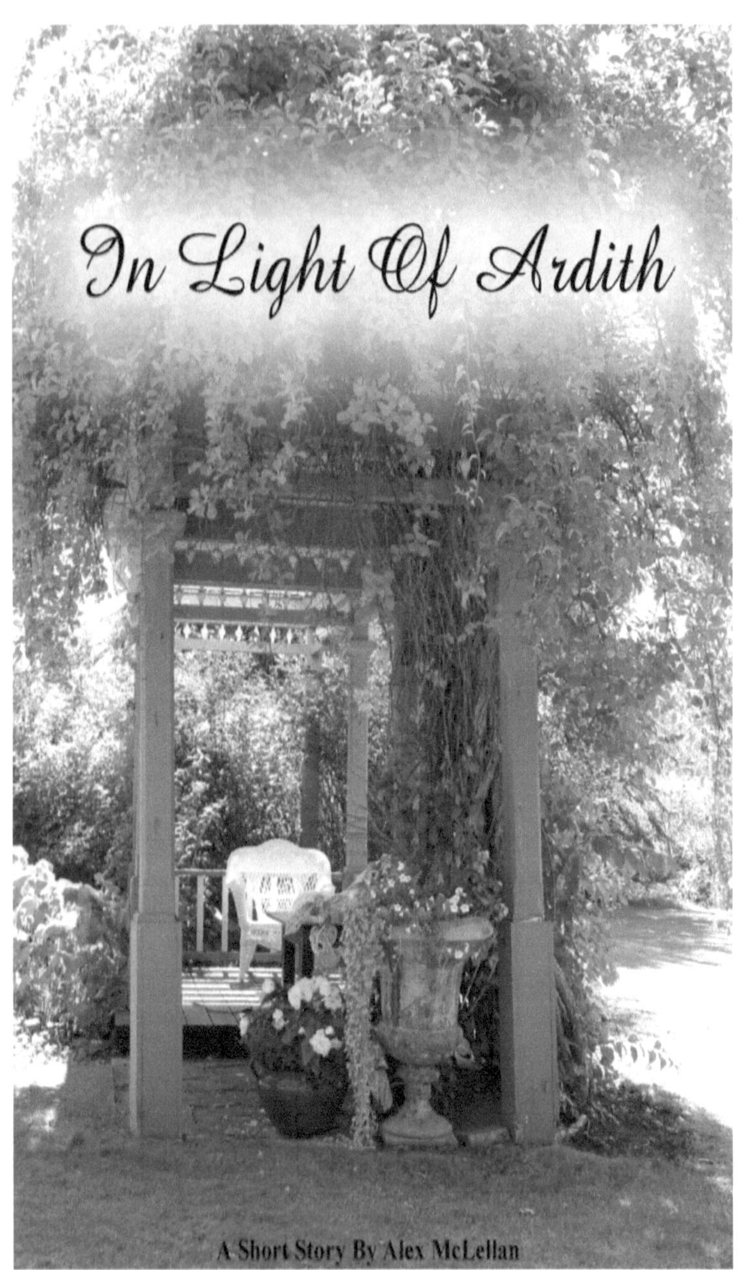

In Light of Ardith

It wasn't until I was explaining to a friend, recounting the story of my parents and the lives they had, that I began to understand, the entirety of what I had seen all my life, was a lie. I mean, I was present but I couldn't see what was right in front of me. Perception and interpretation, and now, I have regret.

Ardith was, is, was my mother, Ardith Noble. She died two weeks ago, a long time sufferer of Alzheimer's. Ardith was the mother of four, wife and widow to scientist, inventor, Elgin Noble. I suppose Ardith was relatively young to develop Alzheimer's as typical Alzheimer patients usually present in their later years, Ardith was only in her forties when the signs started to surface. My father, refused to see the signs and the illness ravaged our family, tore apart relationships, and created deep irreparable damage, especially for my brothers and my younger sister. My father bore the brunt of that hostility.

As the years went by, he kept Ardith home and this created a bone of contention between all of us. Everyone had an opinion. Everyone knew what was best for my mother and Elgin had the final word. Often, according to care Nurses,

Elgin submerged himself in his work and on occasion, days would pass when he hadn't even seen Ardith. That whole time of our lives was heart wrenching.

While my mother suffered and quickly we became strangers to her and each other, marriages resulting in grandchildren Ardith would never know, never hold, and never love, would come to pass and Elgin just deteriorated submerging himself in his secret projects, seeking solace in his work.

Alex, my eldest brother often argued with Elgin. Shouting matches, well Alex shouted and Elgin kept quiet mostly, lost in his own world of inventions and science and for Elgin, time would pass that way. Alex would call and ask how the shell of his mother was doing and Elgin would answer, "Remarkably interactive, quite pleased. All in good time, my dear boy, all in good time."

We often heard Alex shout, "What the hell does that even mean? All in good time?!"

Alex called Elgin a selfish bastard, saying Elgin never had a thought for anyone other than himself the whole of his life and suspected he ordered us children online or grew us in a pod or petri dish because Alex couldn't imagine Elgin actually, physically loving Ardith in any sort of familiar manner that would produce children.

Before our mother had Alzheimer's she would correct us and re-enforce the idea that our father loved us very much, explaining he had his own way and she loved that about him. She always told us not everyone is the same and we shouldn't expect to always understand choices other people make.

Ardith filled her days raising us, volunteering, quilting, knitting, taking care of Dad, making sure he ate, and slept. Each new invention, each new discovery brought us more wealth, which was inconsequential to him most of all, followed by Ardith who simply banked everything, and was also disinterested in money.

She always told us when we argued and especially at dinner, "What's the point of having all this money if we don't have each other? So silly, now eat your vegetables."

That was a typical argument with our mother. If we wanted something, we could earn it, pay for it ourselves. This was so irritating for us as children who often witnessed our mother giving away heaps of money to the food bank and other charities, but that is how she and my father thought it best to raise us, teaching us the real workings of the world.

It was the garden that pre-occupied Ardith's life and she was happiest in her garden. Planning walk ways, garden paths, planting, moving plants, growing the most beautiful roses, and then there was the secret garden, which was not a secret to us, it was just a tall hedgerow where she planted her absolute favourite roses and unique variety of English garden specialties. She often spoke of how the light fell on different parts of the yard during different times of day, saying it was like God wanted us to see everything magnificently highlighted, allowing us to see everything miraculous life had to offer.

It is very difficult when a person's outside does not contain the person you know and love within. That person simply doesn't exist anymore. It's so strange to look at the person, in our case, our mother, and know she is not to be found in those eyes, her light, gone.

We, the kids, that is, came to refer to Ardith as Pre-Ardith and Ardith-Now to avoid confusion in the event we wanted to ever reminisce as we didn't meet regularly.

There was so much resentment. When Elgin died before my mother, he died alone in his lab at home, in front of the computer he invented, that no one else knew how to use. He was not with my mother. He did not say good-bye. He died with what he loved more than life I supposed, his work.

My youngest sister attended Elgin's funeral along side of me as a show of support. Our brothers did not attend. My sister had to wear a brave face because she felt she was robbed the most by the Alzheimer's that ravaged our mother and being youngest, was forgotten most by Ardith during family visits. In her mind, she had the least amount of time with Pre-Ardith and always felt Elgin didn't care if she herself were dead or alive. That was Leesa's burden and she felt it most acutely on so many levels. Alex, well, he's been bitter forever. Ardith was a best friend to Alex, an eldest son who loved his mother, admired her strength, and faulted her for a poor choice of husband and father to her children. Alex would have walked through fire for Ardith. Alex married Gwyneth and loved her like a queen. They made the rest of us nauseous with their undying romantic, dramatic devotion. Still, they were dedicated and they loved each other through six children. Then there was my other brother, Thomas. Thomas was sweet, kind and forgiving. He became the glue that held us together and refused to hate, blame or mistrust. Thomas married his high school sweet heart and they had four kids, much like the life we grew up in, except that he is a very hands-on father, involved. I got married too, to Lawrence. We have two children, Margaret, Maggie for short, and Ethan. Leesa is married and expecting her first child.

Following the death of Elgin, we took mandatory guilt turns visiting Ardith and as time passed, we grew so very tired with the travel, the lack of Ardith's acknowledgement, the sorrow, mourning a shell of person who had already gone, but was still alive. It was horrible, emotionally debilitating and horrible. We felt it best at this point not to remove Ardith as her conditioned worsened.

Ardith passed away precisely one month to the day after Eglin, as in right down to the very minute, on the same day of the very next month. The in-home nurse said that sometimes that happens when people are in love. Alex said it can also happen when people are accustomed to being ignored and detested and when that person dies, what's left to live for?

Following Ardith's funeral, we were forced to think about the house which Alex wanted to sell

at auction in its entirety and be finished with it.
Not one of us entered Ardith's room, we just
couldn't. Thomas wanted to explore and
reminisce, and Leesa didn't have a preference.
For some reason the whole process affected me
in a way most unexpected.

I offered to pack up Elgin and Ardith's clothes,
and went over to the house the day we were to
meet with both the family and estate lawyers.
The house was silent and still except for Ethan
and I. Ethan, just seven, had a lot of questions.

"Why didn't Ardith go to the hospital if she was
so sick?"

"Elgin wanted her to stay here, this is her
home," I tried to sound understanding even
though we all wanted her to be in a proper
hospital.

"Why do you call your parents their names, not
mom and dad?"

"Well, during Pre-Ardith we called them mom
and dad, but when Ardith-Now became sick and
Elgin didn't move her to a hospital, we got
angry at Elgin."

"Maybe Elgin would miss Ardith if she ever went away," Ethan's young mind offered up a possibility to explain Elgin's actions.

"Ha! Fat chance, honey. Elgin hardly ever came out of his lab."

Ethan's face beamed sadness and disappointment.

"I call Ardith, Gramma and I call Elgin, Grampa. They call me, Little E."

"Pardon me?"

"That is what they call me."

"That's nice honey. I like that you think of her that way. I'm sorry she didn't get to know you."

"She knows me and I know her. She knows all of us."

"Ethan, listen. I know you are being very brave and trying to be helpful. Elgin didn't spend any time with you, and I know you think you knew him but honey, you didn't. Ardith suffered from a very bad disease called Alzheimer's, remember? It steals away memories. Ardith didn't remember any of us, honey, it wasn't her fault. I understand you would have loved to know your grandmother, and even your grandfather but it just couldn't have happened. I'm sorry honey. "

Ethan seemed frustrated with me, but respected and accepted my response with a quiet assurance that he was right and I was wrong.

I found myself getting choked up as we entered the wing my father had specially built for Ardith. I held Ethan's hand as we entered the room we had been in just a few weeks earlier to visit the shell of a woman I once knew as our mother. For some reason, perhaps because Ardith was no longer in the bed, I noticed how unusual the room was. Ethan caught my noticing all the buttons and that was when I realized, this was no ordinary hospital bed.

We heard a knock at the door and Helen, one of Ardith's five care nurses, came in.

"Hi there, I've forgotten a few of my books and a couple of things. I saw the car and thought if you didn't mind, I'd stop in for a minute."

"Certainly Helen. How are you keeping?"

"I'm fine, still miss them. Great people your parents. Hi there, Little E."

Helen's greeting made Ethan smile at me in validation.

"You mean Ardith?" I couldn't help myself.

"No m'am. I miss both of your parents. They were so much in love."

I must have given a face that completely revealed my thoughts.

"Oh, that's right, I remember now! You kids haven't been to the lawyer's yet have yah? We'll that will come and you will be so surprised. Your parents are donating this entire facility to Alzheimer sufferers."

"Pardon me? Facility?"

"Oh I know how you kids felt, but those grandchildren of Ardith's meant the world to her," Helen tried to comfort me.

"Helen, even on a good day, Ardith couldn't tell the difference between me and the Pope! She couldn't possibly have known her grandchildren."

Helen looked confused.

She turned to Ethan. "Would you like to show mommy something she needs to see?"

Ethan's face beamed with excitement. So many times I left him with Helen and Ardith while he coloured, or so I thought, and I tried to visit Elgin, tidy Elgin's room, or just try to have a conversation.

That was when it happened. I was perplexed. Ethan giggled, "Watch this mommy!"

Helen cautioned, "Now E, you remember the rules?"

"Yup!"

"Ethan, why don't you show your mom Ardith's Garden?"

He jumped on the bed and sat off to one side when pressing a button on the side of the bed. To my amazement, suddenly everything in the room had changed. Somehow the room had transformed into our childhood home, décor, paint, books on shelves, music, the smell of dinner cooking, and through the living room windows I could see Ardith's beautiful summer garden. But how could this be? It was September, and everywhere else in this part of the county was experiencing Fall. I couldn't believe or understand what I was looking at.

"It's really something isn't it?" Helen commented.

"Helen, I don't understand. We have all been here many times and never noticed?" I asked.

"The mind sees what it wants to see. You saw the program that was familiar to you. Oh there are so many different programs. When Ardith got to the point when she couldn't walk, your father created a walk for her, anywhere she wanted. He even created the sensation of movement so her mind could actually feel like she was moving. "

Ethan was so excited to show me what the "Ethan" button did.

He pressed the button, "Look Mommy! Look!"

When I looked out the window I couldn't believe my eyes.

I wasn't sure that I was not insane, or dreaming, or maybe I was finally able to identify with my mother- OMG ! Maybe I had Alzheimer's!

The experience put me in mind of watching Star Trek where people would go to the hologram deck and the room became an entirely different place. Now the room became three dimensional hologram of Ardith's garden and there she was, sitting on the white chair in her secret garden, and the sun shone on her in all its beauty!

"Hi Gramma!" Ethan hopped off the bed and walked over to Ardith. If that wasn't incredible enough, Ardith was Pre-Ardith, and she turned to Ethan, looked him in the eye and said, "Hello Little E."

"Oh My God! What the hell is happening?" My hands cupped my mouth as my eyes filled with tears. How I missed my mother! Helen walked over to me and said, "It's alright, honey, go on over."

I walked slowly. I was frightened.

So incredible, unbelievable and until that moment I had not realized just how much I wanted my mother back. The hologram turned to me and spoke, "Hello Janey! My, it has been a long time. Your father will be so pleased to see you. "

I could smell the roses from the garden as a breeze floated across my face before I fainted while a favourite childhood memory visited me of my parents walking in the garden.

When I awoke, my siblings surrounded me in the family room. They didn't understand and I didn't have the words. The computer program had returned to the hospital room setting.

Lawrence held my hand and asked if I was ok. "Ethan?" I felt dazed. "I'm right here mommy. Maggie's here too."

Still in shock I looked to my husband, "Lawrence, I remember when I was a kid and my father and mother walked out to Ardith's garden and he did his impersonation of Charlie Chaplin's walk, a shuffle kind of thing and Ardith kicked him in the butt from behind as they kept on walking together, arm in arm. I remember that! I do! What's happening? I haven't thought of that in years! Do you remember?" I looked to the faces of my brothers and sister.

"Yes, so what?" Alex asked. "Listen, one cute little interaction doesn't make up for years of neglect and abuse."

"It's not like that! I saw the room!" I was firm but still dazed whispering in shock.

"Listen, Sis, I know you've had some kind of shock, but the estate lawyer and family lawyer are here. Are you up to it? That's why we're meeting here, remember? Let's get on with it."

"Sure, ok.", but still in shock, my mind raced to all the times Ardith smiled, laughed, and Elgin just looked at her, stared, concentrated intently, making memories, loving her, admiring her with his most serious facial expression. It was not detest, it was love, admiring, a scientific study of his wife and every single aspect about her. My perspective changed and I could actually see for the first time. "He loved her all this time, he really, really loved her!"

"What are you going on about? You know what? Never mind!" Alex said abruptly.

I was frustrated that I couldn't share the experience immediately.

Alex was frustrated and confused, "Look you know I love you, Sis, but maybe you banged your head or something, just pull it together. You are making things harder than they need to be. Now let's get on with it."

We all sat together, each sibling with their spouse and children and Mr. Baxter began.

"I've known you all since you were children yourselves and I have the honour today to share with you the greatest gift a lawyer, dare I say friend to both of your parents, could share with any family, a legacy. "

Baxter teared up.

"When Ardith was diagnosed with Alzheimer's, I never saw a man so destroyed as Elgin. I thought he would do himself an injury just at the thought of losing your mother. Two days after the diagnosis, he came to me and told me what he intended to do, something unbelievable, something never before done, and trust me when I say this, Ardith was in complete agreement. The first thing he did was to convert this estate home into a facility. As you children were so vehemently upset at the time, several months passed and although sad not to have seen any of you very much, he understood what must be done, and both parents agreed the task must be done whatever the cost, even at the expense of your feelings.

What you believe to be your childhood home, is a state of the art facility devoted to Alzheimer's, the understanding of the disease, and Elgin created a treatment that is now proven and will be adopted in facilities like this one across the world. Your father extended Ardith's life while maintaining a quality of life unheard of. He even prepared in the event he died before Ardith. She wouldn't be alone, not for one moment. Elgin had a very good reason for that desire, he was dying you see. Children, your father had Cancer." The room went quiet with shock.

"He knew he had a few short years at best and so as you will understand reflectively, time was of the essence. He always used the expression, 'All in good time,' and now you all will understand, perhaps forgivingly and compassionately, that all time for Elgin was in fact, good. Any moment, any second that allowed him to be on this planet with his beloved Ardith was all that mattered.

This estate is therefore left to the Alzheimer's Society. It's aptly named the, "In Light Of Ardith Foundation."

Baxter was visibly shaken needing a moment and the Estate Lawyer shook Baxter's hand and took over.

"Now, while you are digesting the information so eloquently bestowed upon you, I bring your attention to this," and he, Mr. Ellis pointed to an empty space beside him as though there was a real person standing beside him, ready to be introduced.

That's when it happened. Suddenly a three dimensional solid and exact image arrived and Elgin began to speak to us, all of us, but not before he knelt down on one knee as E ran up to the image, "Hello, little E."

"Hi Grampa Elgin, I missed you."

"I've missed you as well. Did you show your mother the room?"

"Yah, she fainted."

Elgin slapped his thighs and laughed.

Alex looked to me and I punched his arm.

"Now, now, there will be none of that, Janey. Your brother didn't know what he knows now and that is my fault."

Alex sat down because his legs failed him realizing even then, he still didn't know what was happening and we all sat mesmerized. An interactive, three dimensional Elgin, posthumously just as I had seen Ardith, began to explain the impossible.

Incredible, amazing, eternal life and Elgin had managed it.

"I never really told you kids how much I loved your mother and I know I didn't show it to you either. So much happened children.

Let me start at the beginning.

I suppose I must begin with meeting your mother. On the day I met Ardith, the sun was shining like I had never seen it shine before. She sat up upon a brick wall by the ocean and the sun was resting on her back and hair and perfect shoulders, and I stood in absolute awe, which made your mother laugh hysterically. Even her laughter was the most miraculous of sounds to me. I had never seen a living thing as beautiful and inspiring and absolutely perfect as Ardith. I knew in that moment, I would love that woman for however long I remained alive and I knew for certain as the sun shone brightly, I must always stand in the light of Ardith. For that is where I would become real, exist, love and be loved in the light of an Angelic being. Ardith is light, life for me, a scientific anomaly and without her I didn't want to be, even as you children came, more light, each one of you unique and beautiful and filled with the light of Ardith.

I was amazed at the beauty of each one of you, which also made your mother laugh. Ardith understood and loved me even with all my faults. When Ardith was diagnosed with Alzheimer's, I could not believe God would take her from me in this manner, not a heart attack and gone, not a car accident and gone, but gradually and painfully, remove her light, leave me in darkness, leave her in darkness. I couldn't bare it. Not Ardith! Not my light you see, I couldn't leave my children and grandchildren without allowing them to forever see this incredible miracle of life, this beautiful woman, a force to be reckoned with, and I had to share what it feels like to be in the light of Ardith. "

There was not a dry eye in the room. Ethan elbowed me, "Told yah!"

"Yes, you did."

Ellis continued. "A simplistic understanding is to merely say that Elgin had been recording each of your eye imprints, fingerprints, heartbeats, and more information about each and every one of you. He created an interactive program that identifies each one of you when you enter the room, Ardith's room. Elgin created a program that is identical to he and Ardith and their consciousness' in every way. You can have direct conversations with either one at any time and Ardith's room shall never be altered, that is to say the program will never be tampered with. Ardith's gardens have been systematically measured and reproduced right down to scent and breeze during different seasons. Most notably the program is intelligent, self-aware

and is intuitive, responsive. When Ardith
wanted anything, the program responded with
the correct memory, right down to the sound of
birds in the distance, ocean's waves crashing if
she was within a dear memory of an ocean side
vacation. If she had a question or called out to
you kids while lost in a memory, your time
appropriate image appeared to her to converse.
She also enjoyed spending time with your father
in her garden as well." Ellis paused giving the
floor to Elgin.

"Elgin?"

And Elgin continued, "I am sorry. I am sorry for
not spending more time with each one of you
but I can only hope that you get caught up and
visit Ardith's room and speak with us whenever
you wish. I've got birthdays, and Christmas' and
so much more children. I am certain you have
forgotten many things but will be able to see as
your mother and I remember, wonderful,
amazing, special, unique and most of all, love.
You are all loved, even you little one."

The hologram of our father turned to our
youngest sibling. "Your mother felt this most
profoundly and we had to acknowledge her
feelings and mine. Time is such a precious thing
and you children need to know how we loved

you. Alex, my first child, my first son, my Ardith's first miracle of light and perfection and intelligence, so brilliant, I was embarrassed at first to see such an important miracle and be in any small way responsible. I've always felt inadequate to raise you somehow. What could I offer to perfection of grandeur? Then came little Janey, perfect, full of light and love of Ardith and so beautiful, what could I offer? When Thomas arrived I saw light so humble I was ashamed of every wrong doing I may have done, from swatting an insect to breathing, and when finally, little Leesa came along, I was spent. Another little Ardith, another light of being, another miraculous culmination of perfection with as it turns out, humour, and again I thought, me a scientist, what could I offer? I know nothing about children, but Ardith, my rock, my light, would save me. There was enough room in my heart for all of you. Knowing Ardith you see, made me have a heart, become a better man, be human almost. Science took a back seat and I can never explain how Ardith saved me, moved me and brought my heart to the real meaning of life, existing and witnessing the light of Ardith. Remember the reference to light is a scientific symbiotic reference, like language to me, identifying life itself. That is why I keep referencing it in my explanation." Elgin waved us towards Ardith's room.

It's safe to say the four of us ran to Ardith's room leaving the entire family, wives, husbands, kids behind. Alex entered the room first. He spent twenty five minutes. We could hear him speaking with Ardith and Elgin and he came out a changed man. He touched my shoulder on the way out and went straight to our youngest sister.

"Don't be afraid. You know how I hated, yes-hated Elgin, Dad, but I can tell you, this room will change you. Ask anything you like. We can come back any time we like and as often as we want. I can't believe I wasted precious time with Elgin!"

As siblings of Alex, we were amazed, and of course couldn't wait to have our turn.

Hours passed and we returned to Ellis, gob smacked, giddy, silly, enamoured, enriched, and we joined our families as different people than when we left and returned to our lawyer.

Elgin was there to greet us.

"And so now you see, feel, smell and learn my children," Elgin waited patiently.

"Alex, I am so sorry. The fault is mine and mine
alone. Your mother taught you everything. I
learned I had Cancer just before Alzheimer's
began seriously affecting Ardith, so time took
on new meaning for me and I had to work as
fast as I could for as long as I could.

Unfortunately the pace took me away from you
kids and I felt it most profoundly. Ardith
encouraged me to work fast and told me it
would be worth it in the end, even if she and I
were not there to see it. I was able to extend my
life enough to complete my work. Ten years
seemed to pass in a heartbeat."

Alex was crying, wife and children at his side,
but when our youngest sibling returned from
Ardith's room and joined us, it was Elgin who
noticed first.

"Our youngest, so now you know."

"Yes father."

"And?"

"And I am so grateful to know I was loved from
the very moment you knew about me to the
moment I was born! I never knew! I'm sorry! I
always thought I was the biggest mistake! Now

I know!" Leesa cried a lifetime's worth of tears as her husband hugged her supportively.

Ellis continued, "Though I realize the situation is critical and unlike I have ever dealt with legally, the room will be sealed forever if all four of you are not in agreement."

We looked at each other and seemed confused by the lawyer's statement.

"Your father wasn't certain how you would take this news," and Ellis looked to Alex.

"Listen I'm fine. I could have been fine for years if I only knew my father loved my mother, even a little all these years, but I am so happy to know he loved Pre-Ardith and Ardith. He's my hero, the real deal! What he did for her, to help her during this time, to care and love like this even after he died, when she may have otherwise been frightened, confused, feeling alone, there are not words."

I shook my head in grateful disbelief.

We now needed time. A second lawyer meeting was scheduled and we went to our homes, elated, exited, confused, and happier than we had been in several years.

When we met next, all that needed to be discussed was funds and none of us were interested. We all wanted all funds to follow our parent's vision and forever allow us to visit with our parents.

When I brought Ethan back again, he rushed to Ardith's room. He was quite eager to find out what if anything was different, now that everything was different, and it seems like all secrets had been revealed.

"Grama Ardith? Are you here in your garden?"

"Yes, over here! Can you smell that, Little E?

"Yup, what is that Grama Ardith?"

"It's yes, not yup, and that smell is fall, Little E. Fall is in the air. We need to start thinking about thanksgiving dinner."

"Oh, like Turkey and stuff?"

"Absolutely!"

"Oh, mum is just outside, I'll tell her."

"No need to tell her Little E. I'll speak with her, love you young man, now go study for your math test!"

"What's wrong Ethan? " I asked.

"Holy smokes! This computer program doesn't miss a thing! Is this what Grama was like with you?"

"Worse!"

Ethan shook his head and walked down the hall.

I entered slowly this time. I wondered what my computer generated mother would have to say to me. "Hello Janey. Happy pre-Thanksgiving."

"Hello Pre-Ardith."

"Yes, I know you called me that. I'm different now you realize."

"Yes, very different,"

"Seriously? You cheeky girl!"

"But what else could you possibly want? You are already eternal."

"Eternal? What do you mean?"

"Uhm,.. What do you mean?" I asked jokingly as I realized then the computer version mum didn't realize she had passed.

"Uhm, alrighty then, we'll work on that!" I was just trying to deflate the situation.

"Don't forget the squash soup!"

"Oh, I'll be sure to bring it."

In Ardith's light there was no version of any world in any dimension that could exist without Elgin, Alex, me and the others. That is how they both wanted it. When as predicted, Dad died first, he had managed to squeeze out more years than expected which is how he was able to finish his work. By that time, Ardith could speak with whomever she wanted through the intricate computer program, visit her garden, her grandchildren, and spend time with Elgin.

Helen, her nurse, reported Ardith never, not even once showed any indication of loneliness, was never frightened in her confusion, never alarmed that something wasn't right in her environment because all changed continuously, repeatedly if needed, a continuous source of computer generated comfort and care. This contribution to Alzheimer patients' quality of life was astounding. The impact on families around the world was overwhelming. The program could also evolve introducing new generations to the program, preparing Ardith and Elgin to become great–great grandparents as time passed.

But for me, there was a special treat waiting. The computer program was listening and when I was about to say goodbye to Ardith, I felt a little sad that as real as the program was, it wasn't the same as the real thing.

"You heading out?"

"Yes mum. Can I get you anything?" I suppose it was just habit that I asked.

"Oh I'm fine honey, just going to take a walk in the garden with your dad."

Ardith called to Elgin and on cue, Dad appeared.

He waved to me, blew me a kiss, took Ardith's arm and began his rendition of Charlie Chaplin's walk. Ardith shouted back to me, "Good bye Janey. See you soon, my dear!"

And Ardith back kicked Elgin in the bum as they carried on walking away from me, arm in arm, down the path towards the sunlight.

I leaned against the door to Ardith's room watching my parents enjoy their stroll as they had done in life countless numbers of times until faded out of view into the sun lit path and sky. I pressed the button to end program and that was when I realized Elgin had actually achieved his ultimate goal for Ardith. What he hadn't realized was how wonderful it was to have him in our lives, really have him, even as a computer program. Elgin's love for our mother, not only returned our mother to us, but gave us our father as well.

Forever he and all our family could live in light of Ardith and what a bright light it is.

Ironic somehow..

While Alzheimer's steals away memories, Elgin discovered a way to return them. It's so comforting to know Ardith passed, still living her cherished memories, a dream come true, an unbelievable, wonderful and full of wonder, dream come true.

 Maybe life is exactly like the song says, "Merrily, Merrily, Merrily, Merrily, Life Is But A Dream."

The End

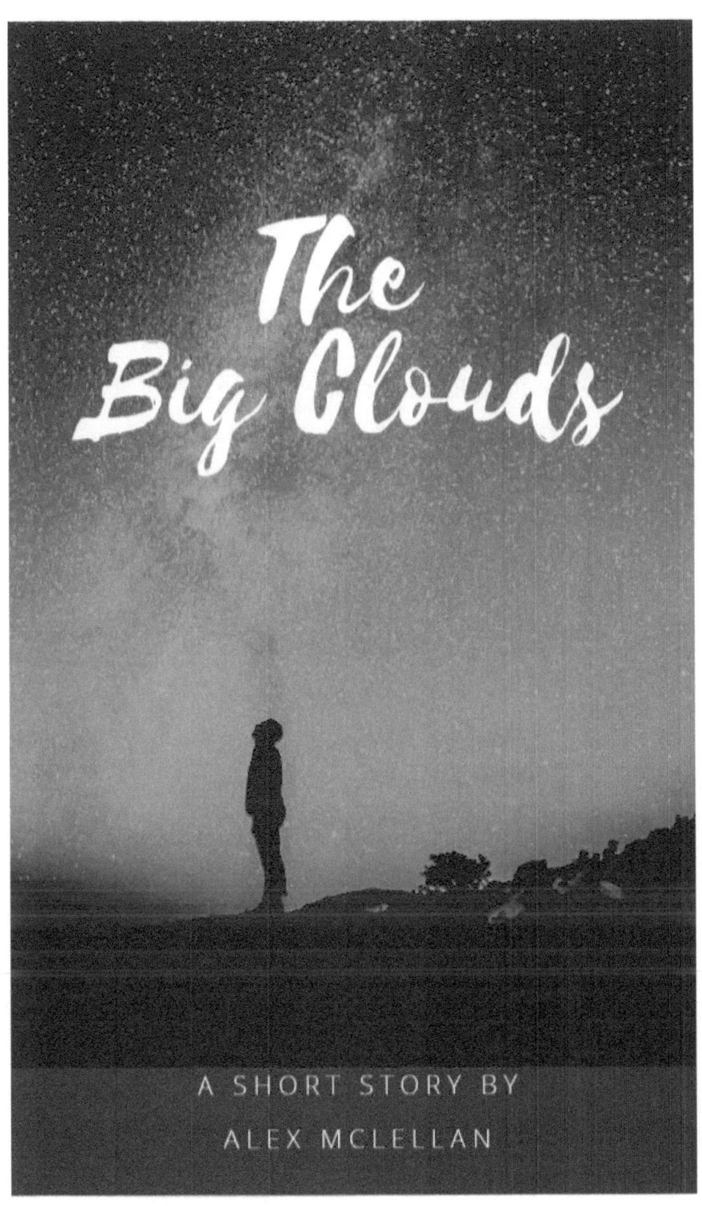
The
Big Clouds
A SHORT STORY BY
ALEX MCLELLAN

The Big Clouds

The boy sat on the beach, bum buried comfortably in the purple sand. His hair now dried and brittle blew furiously in the strong wind, his tattered clothing seemingly unimportant when regarding the layers of dirt over the rest of him.

He had risen early that day and rushed down to the beach to collect all the scraps of paper he could find. He then went in search of charcoal remains from fires the night before. Now comfortable, he sat with charcoal and paper in hand. With a deep cleansing breath he began his sentimental task. He began writing a letter.

'Dear Grampa,

I really miss you. Sorry I haven't written. With everything that's happened, I'm sure you understand. Been thinking I'd like to visit, but everything is so different these days.

Finally the sun is shining again. Now we can measure time. I think I'm a year older since everything began. People are outside again, Gramp. Guess the danger is gone now that the sun is back.

George, this really smart man in our square, tells me that we all have to start over again. Maybe by the time I have grandchildren the water will be blue again and the sand will go back to brown.

Mom doesn't say much these days. I'm sure she sends her love. She was an outsider, Grampa. She wears a scarf on her face all the time. She's all burned. I think it bothers her more than Dad being gone. He was outside somewhere too. We haven't seen him so we guess he's dead like the others. Mom was lucky, but you'd never know it.

George says we can't eat the vegetables that mom has been trying to grow. They come out funny look'n anyway. I tell her not to feel bad about it. I hate vegetables.

George says the whole world is different now. He says something happened to everyone and we'll never know for a very long time. The only good thing is that everyone left is from all over the place and there can't be a war anywhere now. There's no one to fight because there's hardly anyone left and we have to work together now. That's what George says. He's very sad a lot. He lost his whole family being they were outsiders. He's taken a shine to mom and me but it's not the same as talking to you.

Sometimes I dream. I dream I'm visiting you. I dream I wake up to the smell of Grama's breakfasts. It's nice. Then I wake up. My leg doesn't work too well these days Gramps. Mom says I take after you. She reckons I've got 'arther-i-t is', whatever that is. George says that if it gets infected, he might have to take it off. George was a doctor. No more buildings around anymore. That should make a country man like you feel alright. Only thing is there are no more trees anymore either, well hardly any and the ones that lived are burned and stumpy. We'll be o.k. soon.

Now that the sun has come out, I'll write to you once a week. Give my love to Grama.

XOXO Jeremy"

He crumpled the paper, bound it tightly with stray hemp, and drew on it a forty-seven cent stamp. He raised himself upon his makeshift walking stick that he used as a support crutch, and limped off.

George protectively looked on from a distance and began to follow the boy. He followed behind for an hour as Jeremy painfully limped, determined to complete his important task. When Jeremy reached his destination, he tried to balance himself at the same time as putting the letter into the warped, rusted, and burned mailbox which stood alone on the horizon.

"Need a hand young man?" George cheerfully offered.

"George? What are you doing here?" Jeremy was surprised.

"Your mom sent me to look for you."

"She worries too much! She'll never be the same."

"Few things will. Did you write a letter, Jeremy?"

"Yah, to my Grampa."

Jeremy continued to struggle with the warped door of the mailbox. Frustration followed as impatience quickly beamed fury across his face.

"It's been about a year now, George."

Jeremy huffed continuing to struggle with mailbox.

Finally, George could wait no longer.

With sorrow in his voice, "Here, you put the letter in and I'll hold the door open."

George was quick to notice the charcoal drawn stamp. But Jeremy quickly looked at the oozing, infected blisters on his leg. For a fleeting moment, the two caught each other's gaze and just as quickly, they looked away.

Jeremy gently allowed the letter to fall, hitting the empty bottom of the mailbox. After a brief moment of silence, Jeremy blurted out, "I used to write him every week, George. When I was real young, he and I would walk and talk forever about anything. I remember one time, we lay beside each other in the long grass and we stared into the big clouds. Those were the days, George, the days when there were big clouds in the blue sky." Jeremy had chopped breath and tears welled in his eyes as the boy became overwhelmed by this situation.

"Indeed, they were." George could only answer in a whisper as he looked on the now naked and raped environment trying to imagine Jeremy's grassy, cloud filled memory at his grandfather's side. The boy's mental anguish made George long to have his own family near once again even for a moment. What he wouldn't give for even just a moment.

Jeremy, still leaning on the mailbox began to mount the crutch under his arm. He then caught George looking at his leg again. In a sad and quiet voice, George couldn't help but wonder about the boy's well-being, his struggle to part with a life gone forever and while he firmly closed the mailbox door, he compassionately asked, "Jeremy, you do realize…?" George's caring disposition required him to know if Jeremy understood his letter could never be delivered and George also wondered if the mere gesture could be enough to sustain the ten year old while processing the almost impossible heart break of experiencing such devastation.

"Yes, George," Jeremy spoke softly.

George then glanced at the boy's leg a third time knowing the walk must have been incredibly painful. Unable to escape George's notice, Jeremy wiped a single fallen tear from his young cheek, sniffled and swallowed hard.

"I know George, I know," Jeremy answered in a soft voice, sadly and bravely.

And the dishevelled shapes could be seen walking slowly over the purple sand, away from a landscape housing only a single surviving beat up mailbox, into a landscape where barely anything had survived except for a horizon in a hopeful sky without any clouds at all.

The End

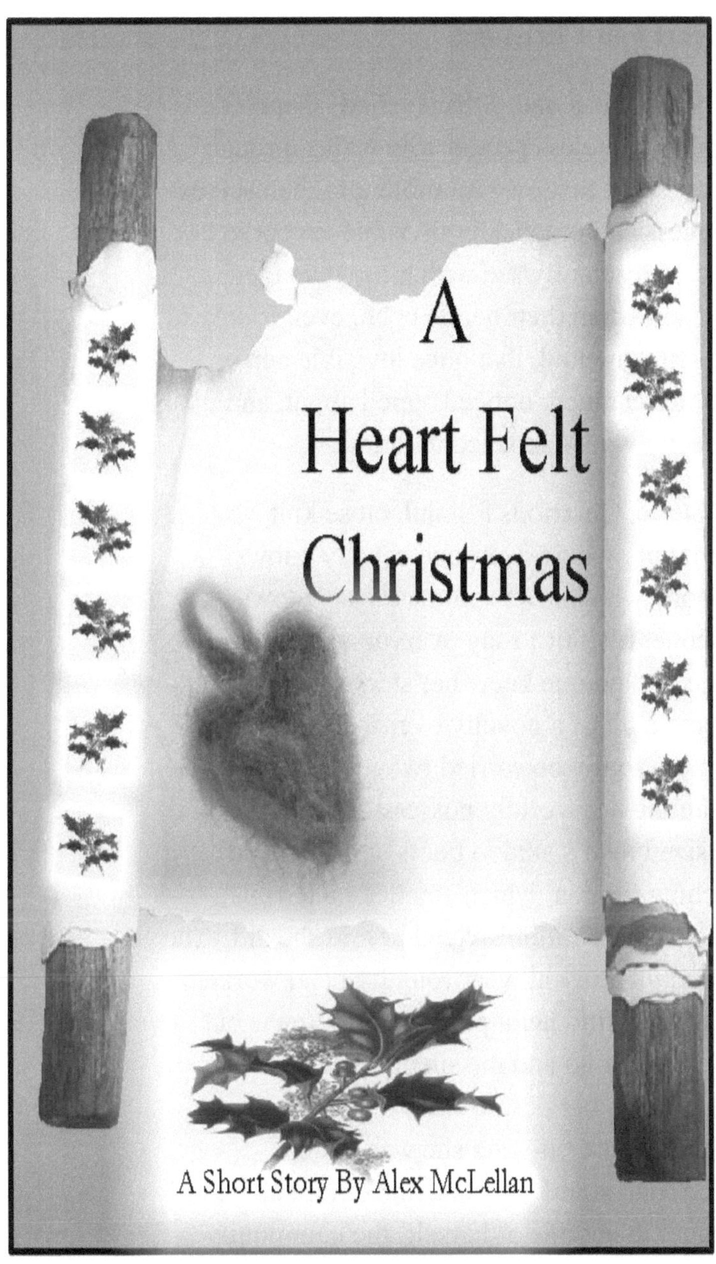

A
Heart Felt
Christmas
A Short Story By Alex McLellan

A Heart Felt Christmas

Every town has one, a dishevelled, shapeless, possibly homeless person who walks through the streets of the town mumbling to themselves. Harmless and practically invisible except to those who actually see with more than their eyes, and when their hearts open, even if only to not be judgmental, that once invisible person becomes claimed, noticed, cared about, and that is exactly what happened to Annie.

Shelburne, Ontario is a small, close knit community where everyone usually knows someone who knows someone who knows someone. It's fair to say everyone knew of Annie, but no one knew her story. She had become a bit of a novelty over the years, a harmless soul who carried two grocery bags containing her worldly possessions. She wore oversized men's skidoo boots, a fur hat and matching fur coat which smelled so terrible, 'eau de Annie' often arrived before she did. She dressed this way all year round. Social workers had tried to find her a place off the streets but she wouldn't go and missing person reports didn't match her description so authorities couldn't figure out who she was. Annie preferred to wander around and since she wasn't a danger to anyone or herself, the community participated in a collective consciousness of never complaining, always allowing her to sleep where she wanted, gave her food whenever they could and together, kept a watchful eye over her.

Annie had a faraway look about her as though she were trying to remember something and though she never made conversation, she would always nod in thanks for kindness, always paying attention to young Constable Rutledge who seemed to keep an eye on her more than most. Occasionally, Constable Rutledge while on patrol would notice Annie and bring her a hot chocolate and a bagel. Having grown up in Shelburne, he was that caring sort of policeman and that kind of gentleman.

On one particular cold winter's night, Annie was nowhere to be found.

Concerned for her safety in the bitter cold, young Rutledge searched all her favourite sleeping spots, behind the local Laundromat, off to the side of Sawyers Feed Mill, in the door well of the Shelburne Free Press, the back entrance of Woolly's Yarns, until finally, he noticed a large cardboard box draped over a clothing drop off box at the Shelburne Legion. Only Annie's two grocery bags and some burned out papers from firecrackers could be seen. It was at that moment, the young Constable had a sinking feeling in the pit of his stomach. He then noticed Annie's familiar dragging footprints left behind in the snow as Annie had walked towards the local fire department. Constable Rutledge checked in with Fire Chief, Captain Morrell who had not seen her. The footprints continued on passed the Shelburne Arena and on to the graveyard. Heart pounding, he couldn't imagine what would have made her walk all that distance deciding something serious must have happened.

Footprints in the snow lead the young Constable all over the graveyard and by the time he found Annie, he found her lying, freezing, staring at the headstone of Andrea McCree, mother of Annie and wife to Adam. Young Rutledge, reading the head stone noticed all three had died years ago. The Constable quickly knelt down and realized that Annie was trying to tell him something and while he waited for back up, she told a story he could not begin to fathom. She died in his arms before help could arrive, and her very last words whispered were, "I remember now."

Annie's death left more questions than answers for the small community and all of Shelburne mourned the death of this stranger they had watched over, claimed over the years and felt responsible for.

For Constable Rutledge however, the odd set of circumstances surrounding this virtual stranger and her passing, left an inexplicable sadness, a need to know more, and he set out to discover what Annie's story was. When all the pieces were put together, Town Officials decided to gather at Town Hall, invite the Town and tell Annie's story.

Young and old alike gathered during a bright, mild winter's day to hear what had happened to Annie, just five days before Christmas.

Shelburne's Mayor Crewson first addressed the eager crowd.

"People of Shelburne, I think we can say we are all saddened by the death of a stranger whom we came to refer to as Annie. Typically, we never see this sort of thing happen in our fine town and it is due to the kindness of many of you that Annie was able to survive for as long as she did. The kindness extended to Annie by the fine ladies at Woolly's Yarns allowed Annie to give gifts to many of us, myself included, suffice to say," Mayor Crewson paused wiping a tear from his eye as he quickly looked into the palm of his hand at a tiny felted heart.

"Annie will have touched all our hearts this Christmas in the true spirit of Christmas when all is revealed. Now, Constable Rutledge will explain."

The young Constable was visibly upset when he approached the microphone. He looked out over the crowd and began, "When this sort of tragedy occurs, it leaves many questions. I would like to ask you all to look around at each other for just a moment before I begin. Most of you know each other or know of each other. We take our lives for granted in Shelburne, walking down the street, saying 'hi' to people, living in a community where if we went missing, we would be searched for. Annie could have been anyone one of us and when you hear her story, think about the person standing next to you right now and remember life can change in a heartbeat.

Several years ago, when the new development was being built, there was a tragedy on Christmas Eve that left that portion of our town devastated. There were only a few families established in the development by this time and a gas leak resulted in the deaths of a young family, the McCree's who were new to

Shelburne. Some of you may remember it was a very sad time of year as both parents and their young daughter passed away.

Rumbling conversation echoed amongst the crowd as those who remembered discussed with their neighbours.

Constable Rutledge continued. "I found Annie's grocery bags over by the Legion and noticed the firecracker pieces on the snow. I later discovered kids set them off and didn't realize Annie was huddled in the cardboard between the clothing drop off box and the wall. The noise must have startled her. I followed her footprints to the graveyard. I found her just in time to hear her story before she died. I'll do my best to tell you in her own words." Constable Rutledge read from his notes.

"Oh, it's you. I remember now, I do. Christmas Eve, our new house. Adam had a nap before late mass. He surprised me, new fur coat, hat. We couldn't afford it. I slipped on his boots to go out and start the truck and called to Annie to wake up her father and switch the fireplace off. When I got to the truck, I looked back. Annie was in the front window watching for me. She was smiling, explosion from behind her, I see through the front window, coming for her, there's no time, so loud, flames, so big, so fast, the house gone, Annie gone, another bang, knocked me over, I hit my head, black soot, the smell,.. I remember now, I started walking, so cold, wet, dirty, I remember now, my head hurt. I remember Annie's smile...." Annie's breathe was laboured as she continued, "I remember, I lived. See, God spared me. God knew I couldn't live knowing. God knew I wouldn't want to live without them. Don't be mad at the kids. The fireworks. They are good boys. They didn't know I was there. The noise, I banged my head on the cement and I remembered I lived. I remember. I can go home now to my family, I found them, see?" Annie pointed to the gravestones. "I can go, I remember now."

People in the crowd had tears in their eyes. They cried for never knowing Annie mumbled her own daughter's name, it was not her own. They cried for the sad situation that resulted from that tragedy so long ago. They cried for Annie to be re-united with her beloved family which is why she walked to graveyard, to see their names for herself, to understand her memories were real.

Young Constable Rutledge wiped his eye, took a deep breath and continued, "It's upsetting to be sure. You are probably asking how this could happen? There were very few families living there at the time and keep in mind they were new to Shelburne. It was assumed the entire family died in the gas explosion and that fire, it was bad, folks. With no one presumed unaccounted for, there was no need to search for anyone. Family and friends never knew Mr. McCree had surprised his wife with a fur coat and hat and Mrs. McCree had become unrecognizable in a very short time. In a state of shock and amnesia, dirtied, she wandered around our town, never making eye contact and mumbling the name Annie, still wearing her husband's boots and the Christmas outfit from the night of the accident. No one looks closely at a homeless person to see if they recognise them, it just doesn't happen.

Now, Mrs. McCree had a little business she had started earlier in the year before the tragedy. She made felted handbags, hats, bracelets and felted soap covers. For those of you who don't know, felting is a really old process of shrinking knitting. The ladies at Woolly's Yarns often gave Mrs. McCree balls of yarn as an act of kindness. No one ever knew she did anything with the yarn. These are the two bags Mrs. McCree carried around with her. They are filled with little felted hearts. These were her only possessions and she gave them to us.

This woman who some of you called, Crazy Annie, was a woman who had lost her family before her very eyes, lost everything she knew and everything she loved. She had the clothes on her back, the name Annie in her heart's memory and a skill. She had nothing and was still able to thank people in her own way. She often gave me these tiny little hearts she had made out of yarn and since investigating her story, I discovered many of you were the recipients of these keepsakes also."

A heavy silence fell across the crowd as many reached into their jacket pockets. Some kids wore their felted hearts attached to their zippers, some ladies kept their felted heart in their wallets, never realizing the little gifts came from Annie.

"No one ever noticed who had left the little keepsake on door handles, in mail boxes, on car antennas. She truly had nothing folks, was the saddest person inside herself and still she gave. That is what she did and that is who she was, and she was one of us Shelburne, she was.

I see many of you have the little hearts from Mrs. McCree," the Constable looked out into the community he protected, "I know we feel bad about the situation but I want to remind you that many of us went above and beyond to keep Annie-Mrs. McCree safe over the years, so that's a good thing. She told me herself, God spared her by not making her face what happened to her family and that's a good thing too, in its own way. But this year, we have Annie- Mrs. McCree to thank.

This time of year especially, we need to remember the true spirit of Christmas. You might think and feel like you have nothing. Some of you feel so overwhelmed by your lives. I'm here to tell you, you have it all wrong.

Following Annie's example, we have our lives to live, we decide every day how it's going to be lived, and the decision to be a good person, is free. Even as devastated as her life was, as sad as she was, as exhausted and alone as she was, she still managed to do good deeds.

That's the story of our Annie, Shelburne. I'm proud to have known Annie and I'm proud to be a member of this fine community and I want to take this opportunity to wish all of you, in Annie's, Mrs. McCree's honour, a 'Heart Felt Christmas.'

The End

Please Be Assured:

A Heartfelt Christmas is a **complete work of fiction** designed to thank the good people of Shelburne for welcoming me into their community. While some names used in the story are borrowed with permission from actual Shelburnites at the time the story was written, please keep in mind, the story is absolute fiction and is intended to remind people of the true meaning of Christmas. Originally written in 2013, many good people in Shelburne were very upset that this story could have actually happened and contacted me angrily. Though "Annie" has never existed, rest easy knowing the good people of Shelburne have always been.

Alex McLellan

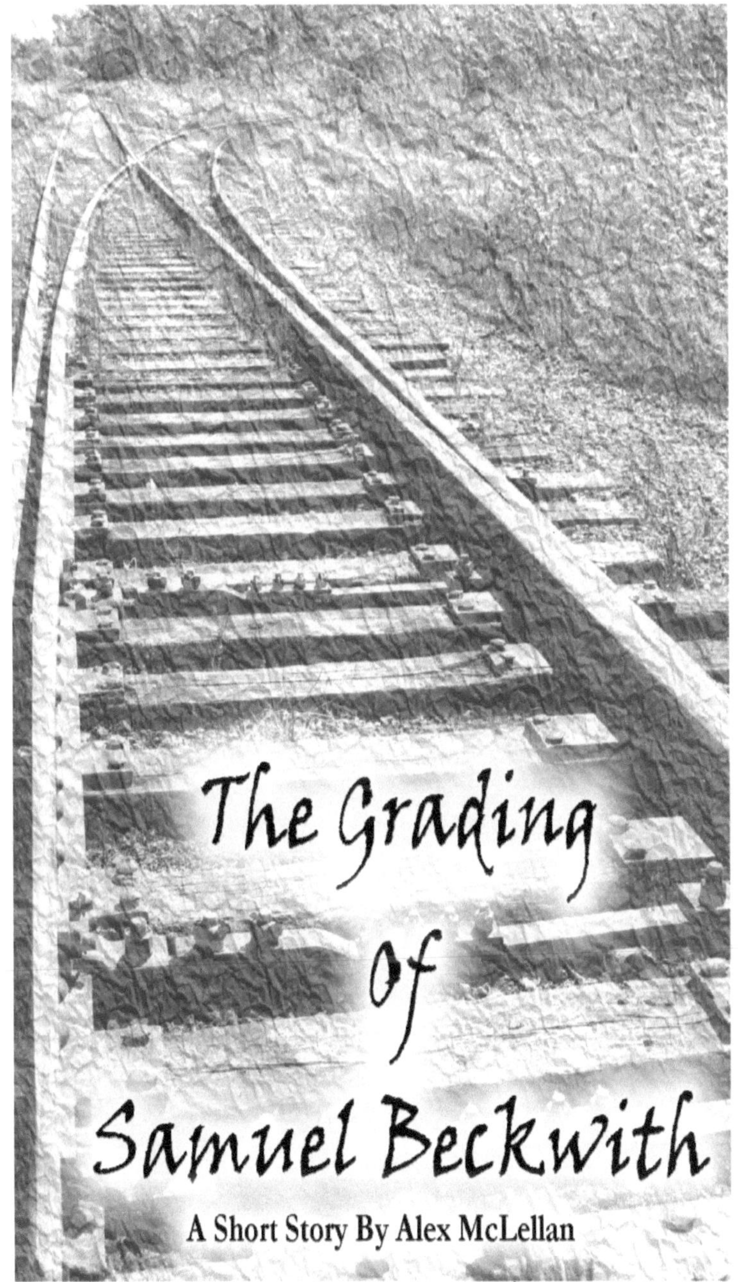

The Grading Of Samuel Beckwith

A Short Story By Alex McLellan

I dedicate this story to my British friends,
Christina and Deb Freeman who always
encourage me to write!

Thank you, my dear friends.

The Grading Of Samuel Beckwith

"It was such a long time ago." The old lady had a tear in her eye as she turned her head and peered out the window from her hospital bed. It was raining that day and her family came for their weekly visit. It was her 24 year old granddaughter who was relentlessly curious, a writer and aspiring documentary film maker who continuously asked about her grandmother's past. They loved each other very much.

"Please Nan, I need to know what happened?"

"Oh Amelia, now? I'm so very tired."

"C'mon, it might feel good to share. I've never heard what happened from your own mouth. It couldn't be easy to keep it to yourself all these years."

"You don't understand how this has haunted me for most of my life. I don't know what really happened, truly I don't. People decided what they thought happened, and I tried, I really tried to explain, but I'll never know what happened. One thing I do know," Beatrice turned to her granddaughter with tear filled eyes, a broken heart and face full with regret, "I know for certain, I didn't save him, you see. Whatever happened to that sweet, little boy rests on my shoulders. I have worn his fate for the whole of my life and I can never forget him. I loved him. I love him still. I would have given my life for him."

Beatrice Freeman, now 85 years old sobbed as though the event happened only moments ago and her granddaughter, Amelia, held her close. Seeing her grandmother cry in that way, Amelia decided there was only so much her grandmother could take, even though Beatrice was a tough old British gal.

"Nan, perhaps we could talk tomorrow when I come back?"

"It's not too late. Perhaps it is the right time." Beatrice began in a chopped breath.

"Only if you are certain. I didn't realize how speaking about it would affect you, Nan."

"It's all about time, my dear. My time will be coming to a close and perhaps this might be freeing somehow."

"I'll record your story," Amelia almost whispered in anticipation of filming and she, herself, also had a secret motive for pressing her grandmother.

The two women made themselves comfortable as Beatrice Freeman's heart unfolded and she began the retelling of the story that forever changed her life. It was a story of lost love, it was a story about a terrible crime, a young boy's future lost, promises made, promises broken, and hope eternal when it was thought all hope was lost. The story propelled Amelia into a distant past, to a time when life itself was very different from her own.

"It was a day like any other day really," began Beatrice, "But more exciting because there was a school trip and it was a two night overnighter and the best part was, it was on a train! My friends and I prepared the children. We were all Nannies you see, on the same street and we were instructed to prepare the children. It was a huge affair. There wasn't one of us Nannies who could have afforded such an adventure. We were giddy as the children. My charge was young, Master Samuel Beckwith. He was eight years old and such a little handful. He was full of life and joy and humour. He was as we Nannies used to say, of good stock. He was kind, honest, and full of integrity. He had dark brown hair and a full head of it. It curled out on the ends and he often became quite upset on that account, not wanting to go to school until I wet it down. I'd been with the Beckwith family for six years and cared for Sam and his young sister, Alexandra, Alley, for short. It was the happiest time of my life. I had broken the rule of not falling completely in love with those two children. As a Nanny, a caretaker must remain detached so to speak, in order to provide the best care for the children making the most logical and standard decisions not governed by emotion," Beatrice paused and peered out the window as though the memories performed live on the street below.

"On that morning, Sam was overjoyed in anticipation. He loved trains and knew most everything about them. The knowledge that young boy retained was astounding to me. He was overjoyed that morning, and threw his arms around me, "Let's go, Nanny B! Let's go! We mustn't be late!"

His parents waved us off so happy to see their young one, admiring the boy he had grown into, and truly thought of me as a member of the family.

Alley waved and shouted, "Good-bye, Sammy! Good-bye, Nanny B!" We marched down the walkway, meeting up with our block of Nannies and their wards, leaving the row of brownstones behind and we were off, children giggling and we nanny's jibber jabbering.

When we arrived at the station, Head Master Jones was there to greet us along with his assistant, Mr. Wenton. Jones astonished we nannies as he brought along the largest carpet bag for a two night trip that we'd ever seen, which prompted a few giggles and eyes back and forth. Head Master Jones was a very tall, thick build sort of man. He had a distinct profile. Mr. Wenton, in contrast was thin, slight in build, with smallish hands, very lady like, and had a very pale complexion, which made his blue eyes very strange somehow to look at, bold and steely, cold as the ocean they were. He was odd and his ears were thick and large, larger than they ought to be, I always thought. My own mother always told me to never trust a man with thick, over large ears and tiny thin hands that never saw a hard day's work in their life. I didn't trust him. It was just a feeing, made the hairs on the back of my neck stand on end.

Noticing our reaction to the abundance of items he brought along with him, Jones commented that unlike the likes of we Nannies, he had real work to do and one can never be too prepared. Jones was always so very condescending, which looking back was expected from a man in his position, I suppose. But that detestable Mr. Wenton, walking around like he had a permanent bad smell under his nose, always rubbed me the wrong way, there was just something about him. I can't explain it really. Too smooth, I thought him at the very least untrustworthy, sly in fact, even shifty.

We each were assigned to our individual sleeper cars and oh my Lord, fancy doesn't begin to describe them! Most of us Nannies didn't come from our own homes as nice as these accommodations. Ah, and wee Sam was over the moon. It was going to be a lovely time.

We were excited, anticipating how the day would unfold expecting breakfast, lunch and tea in the dining car all together. The boys were so fine looking and well mannered, and so sweet in their school clothes. I dare say we were admired by the on-looking passengers, bringing them back to their own school days. The sights we would see, the food we would eat, and the night of sleep and happy dreams was so looked forward to by all. The entire trip would be one we would never forget, like Christmas in spring, it was.

The boys were taken in shifts by Jones and Wenton as they were to each write an essay on how wonderful their train experience was. They met in the dining car, 6 under Mr. Wenton's supervision and 6 in Head Master Jones' private lounge. Jones told the Nannies that this trip is a pilot project, first of its kind, and if all went well, we would be the example, ensuring an annual trip for every student for years to come and as this initiative was his idea, he encouraged all of us to do our best to produce a positive result.

Afterwards, we all met in the dining car to collect our charges. I can't explain it but a heavy mood hung over the boys. A heavy sadness of sorts fell on everyone except Head Master Jones and Mr. Wenton.

We gathered the boys and went to our sleeping cars and began to get the boys settled in when Nanny Nancy knocked at my door. She was very concerned and asked me to step outside, closing the door behind me.

"Beatrice, something terrible has happened! My Algie tells me someone has hurt him. He won't say who, but the boy's a mess, he's absolutely in shock!" Nanny Nancy almost frantic, explained.

"One of the other boys?" I asked. I knew each of the twelve boys and none of them were mean spirited.

"He wouldn't say. He says he can't."

"Can't or won't?"

"Can't and won't. You know the boys are thick as thieves! They'll never turn on one another! But this is,.. something different. The boy's got the fear of the Devil inside him! Oh another thing, he's bruised on his tail bone, like he's had a terrible fall." Nancy was so very worried, understandably so. Our one job is to protect the children in our care.

"I'll check Sam. Meanwhile mention it to the other girls. We'll need eyes open in the back of our heads tonight," I told her.

"That night, I couldn't sleep a wink. I wanted to know why my Sam, my dear heart was so quiet, but he revealed nothing. On the off chance he didn't know about Algie, I wouldn't want to put a spanner in his day tomorrow, but something wasn't right, and I couldn't shake the feeling.

I could hear his little footsteps come close to my bed, "B, are you awake?"

"Yes Sam, what is it?"

"Can I sleep beside you?"

"Is everything alright?"

"Well, we are far from home and it has been a long day," Sam hesitated.

"Ah, course, my sweet boy. Is there anything you would like to talk about? How was your essay?"

"I think I like planes from now on, B."

There was a heavy silence.

"Right. C'mon then, spill! You know I can always tell when something is on your mind."

"Well, I was just wandering what you would have done when you were a child, in the way of defending yourself in a fight."

"That's not really bed time talk, now is it?"

"Well, you are supposed to protect me, right?"

"Yes."

"But you can't be with me all of the time, right?"

"True."

"Well, didn't you have fights when you were young?"

"Well, the place I'm from and the place you're from are very different, young Sam."

"Can you teach me something?" The boy sounded desperate in his plea of inquiry.

"Has someone tried to hurt you or one of the other boys?"

Sam went very quiet. His little chest was pounding in anticipation of some sort of help. So I told him what I'd do.

"Alright then, but this tactic is only to be used under extreme life and death sort of circumstances. Do you know why I keep my keys round my neck?"

"So you don't lose them?"

"So they are handy in case I need to defend myself from pirates or monsters and the likes."

"Pirates? Monsters?" Sam's big brown eyes seemed wider in the moonlight and he smiled.

"See?" I reached for my keys by my bedside table. "If ever someone attacked me, especially a scary pirate, I would grab my key, force it into

the palm of my hand, and in between my fingers
and punch, kick, scratch and scream as though
my life depended on it."

"Would you do that to save me and Alley?"

"Without missing a heartbeat!"

"I love you B."

"I love you too, young Sam. You know you can
tell me anything right?"

"Yes, but Pirates?" Sam smiled.

"I know it's against the odds, but like Jones and
his enormous carpet bag, one can never be too
prepared."

Sam chuckled but I could tell he knew
something was wrong. We neither of us slept a
wink that night, not really.

Breakfast in the dining car was not like the day
before. All the boys were tired and barely
touched their food. We nannies gathered at the
one end, with eyes on our boys and discussed
what we thought was happening but couldn't
figure it out.

More work on their essays, lunch, final work on
their essay, then tea, and then it was final

meetings to review their final projects discussing which essay was the most informative, then off to bed, but this night was very strange. All of us Nannies had our dander up. We were sticking to our boys like glue. They were never unsupervised, they were escorted to the Lu, to the Head Master and Mr. Wenton and back, so we couldn't figure it out.

Algie seemed to be the worse for wear and Nanny Nancy asked if there was a doctor on the train. Following Algie's examination the doctor reported Algie had a fall, was bruised and may have a slight concussion from the fall, which is why Algie couldn't remember how it happened.

Sam was scared. I had never seen him like this, silent and filled with dread. Nancy came to my room with Algie and she and I took turns watching the boys while we visited the Lu and washed up.

Nancy was very worried. She said the boys looked at each other knowing a secret, but never spoke the whole time I was away. It was the same when she left us.

For some reason, Sam was very keen to know the time that night and asked every ten or fifteen minutes, like he was waiting for something to happen. He began to get panicky as nine o'clock approached and was sitting straight up.

There was a knock at the door and Nancy whispered, "Beatrice, let me in! It's Algie!"

I leapt up to the door of our sleeper car. Nancy was crying. "Algie's wet the bed! He won't stop crying. I stripped the bed and changed it but I've got to wash out his bottoms. Come to my room and bring Sam?"

I grabbed Sam by the hand and he grabbed my chain with my keys, giving it to me and when we arrived at Nancy's sleeper car, just a few cars over from ours, there stood Algie almost as in a trance, tears just streaming down his wee face. His night shirt covered his privates and he stood in a puddle of urine as he stared straight forward, standing beside the bed linen which Nancy had hurriedly replaced and left in a pile on the floor. Nancy grabbed his bottoms and I helped him to his bed. Sam sat beside Algie and they held each other's little hands, which surprised me to see at this age, expressing that kind of affection and worry for each other. Nancy stood up in shock and horror, letting out a gasp. Algie gripped Sam's hand tightly, still staring straight ahead.

"Oh my good God! Beatrice look!" On the inside of the back of the bottoms was a small trickle of blood. She rolled the bottoms into a ball, turned and kissed Algie on the forehead. "Oh my sweet, sweet boy, what has happened to you?!"

"Nancy I'll stay, you fetch the doctor immediately."

Nancy rose quickly. "Show him the bed clothes and tell him he must come immediately to tend to the boy," I told her.

"Do you think he's been poisoned?" Nancy's mind searched for the extreme, some sort of explanation.

"I can't say, hurry!"

Truth was, I didn't know. It was only a matter of minutes that had passed when it happened. I looked over at Sam, who stared at Algie, his best pal since birth, and Sam was so frightened.

"Don't worry, Sam. Algie will be alright." I leaned in and kissed Sam on the forehead. Remember our little chat last night?"

Sam nodded.

"Good then!" I was impatient and frightened.
"Where is Nancy with that Doctor?!" I
whispered to myself.

I poked my head out the car and to my surprise,
there was Mr. Wenton.

"Oh! I dare say you startled me, sir!"

"Nanny Beatrice, I just bumped into Nanny
Nancy."

Mr. Wenton brushed by me and went to Algie.
"Poor lad! Perhaps it's all the excitement. Hello,
Sam."

Untypically, Sam didn't answer.

Mr. Wenton, brushed by me again on his way
out and standing in the door way turned to me,
"Nanny Beatrice, please let me know if you or
any of the other Nannies need my help caring
for the boys during this troubled time."

As he turned and walked away, I heard a
tremendous thud. I was frightened to lean out
the door to take a peek, but I finally mustered
the courage. Holding Sam's hand I stretched
and leaned, almost crouching. I poked my head
round the corner to the right to see Mr. Wenton
on the floor. Then suddenly I felt a huge pain to
my side of my head and a strange pull on my

neck like a cut and that's all I remember. I have no idea how I got back to my room, must have stumbled back in a daze, but when I opened my eyes, Sam was nowhere to be found, and I had a huge gash on the side of my head, dripping with blood and a bruising round my neck with a slight cut that bled onto my uniform.

I was panicked! My Sam was gone! I made my way to Nancy's car, still bleeding and I must have looked a sight. The doctor who had been tending to Algie immediately took hold of me and sat me down. I was almost fainting, "Where's my Sam! My Sam is gone!"

Nancy was inconsolable. She flung her arms around me. "Oh, Beatrice, my poor Algie, now your Sam!"

Algie sat in a complete state of shock, silent, wide eyed, staring straight ahead, shiver'n.

"Madam, this boy has been sodomized! I demand to know what is going on here!" the Doctor announced.

I looked over at Algie and saw he sat in a trance-like state, the boy was unable to speak.

The pain in my head was overpowering. I wasn't sure I heard properly over Nancy's tears.

"I, I, I beg your pardon, come again?" I asked the doctor.

"Buggered! The boy's been buggered!" Nancy shouted, near hysteria with grief.

I fainted after that and when I came round, I was in hospital and the investigation was full on. The Beckwith's had my things removed from the house, wanting nothing more to do with me. I was in pieces. I've never recovered fully. In the next few days, Head Master Jones was arrested for tampering with the boys, eleven out of twelve of them, Sam among them but not included in the charges only because Sam was never found. Some people thought I killed him! For many years I was a suspect. Some even to this day think I'd rather have killed the boy than lose my job, claiming innocence and ignorance. None of it mattered, only my Sam mattered to me."

Beatrice paused.

"Is that why father is named, William Samuel?" Amelia asked.

Beatrice nodded while wiping her eyes.

"Oh Nan, you've carried this guilt all these years? That's why father taught me the key thing, for safety?"

Beatrice nodded again.

"I always held out hope Sam survived somehow, that he wasn't dead. Strange how when your grandfather passed, I felt it was so, God bless him. But I never have had that feeling with my Sam. Now as my years come to an end, I'll never know what happened. His family will never know, even Jones never admitted to any of it. I never trusted Jones, but didn't think him capable of that. You know, that awful Wenton carried on in Jones' place for years before retiring. I never liked him. I always thought he knew more than he was fessing up to."

"So the case was never solved?" Amelia's reaction was incredulous.

"No, my dear. Sad but true. Scotland Yard thought that Jones had hit me on the head and taken Sam, and even went so far as to think I may have been in on the whole plot."

"A real life mystery, Nan!"

"Yes indeed."

Amelia offered to get her Nan tea, made her comfortable for the night.

Truly, Amelia had been studying the case for years. She had been searching for answers, conducting interviews, researching, discovering leads. Finally, Amelia had stumbled onto something very curious to her while searching. She had discovered records of boys shipped out of England during that time, orphans and other boys whose families were hoping for them to have a better life abroad and the likes. They were referred to as British Home Boys. One such boy named, an orphan, Ben Algiers took a voyage to Canada the same year as the incident. He was to become a farmer's ward on a place outside of what was then referred to as Toronto, Canada. Ben Algiers was seven or eight years old. Doing some math, Amelia desperate to clear her grandmother's name and give her some peace, realized that Ben Algiers would now be in his late sixties. The hunt for answers was on!

It would take only a month for Amelia to decide she would visit Canada. Amelia knew this trip was a huge leap of faith, but in her heart of hearts, she had to try. She made her Nan promise to be alive when she returned, but never explained the true reason for her videoing her grandmother, her quest for truth, and never mentioning the gut feeling that she was really onto something.

Amelia was surprised to see how similar Canada was to parts of England and Scotland. Her search took her to Dufferin County, British Home Children directories, and finally she discovered that Ben Algiers, the scared little boy who travelled from England became Bartholomew Woods, and still lived on the Woods' family farm, just outside of Orangeville, Ontario.

Amelia brought her video camera, went to the farm hoping to find him and get live footage. She was scared and emotional to bring up this entire history from so long ago but had decided to not call ahead hoping the surprise might bring answers if this man was the gentleman she searched for. Amelia's hope was second only to her anxious anticipation of this meeting and the suspense was almost unbearable because of the unfathomable possibility that this man was not the man she searched for.

She approached the front door of a beautiful farmhouse and an older gentleman came into view, peering into the glass door window. A very pretty, older woman followed behind and when the gentleman opened the door, to Amelia's horror, the gentleman grabbed his chest, turned and went to sit immediately on a kitchen chair.

"Bart, now what's gotten into you? You look like you've seen a ghost! Please come in young lady and close the door behind you."

"B!?" Bart whispered in disbelief looking at Amelia.

"Now you're starting to make me think you are having a stroke? B?" his wife asked.

"Not B. I've been told I bear a striking resemblance. I'm B's granddaughter. I am Amelia, and I think I'm in the right place," Amelia beamed with satisfaction and relief.

"Bart? What's going on here?" His wife had never seen him in such a state.

Amelia apologized for the shock and after some tea, Bart was recovering nicely and the explaining and catching up could begin.

"I am here on behalf of my grandmother. You may have known her as, Nanny Beatrice? Does that ring a bell?"

Bart's lips quivered. He then held his head in his hands and began to weep like the child he truly was, the child who had lost everything.

"What in heaven's name is going on?" asked his wife.

Bart ushered Amelia towards him. He held her close. "B is real! You look like your grandmother. I'm almost certain B saved my life!"

It took several moments for Bart to compose himself. To his wife's complete astonishment, he then rose and returned with a rather large carpet bag, still sobbing.

"Oh my god! She is real! She WAS REAL! Amelia, B, Nanny Beatrice saved my life. It's all true! I wasn't sure until seeing you right now if the whole thing was a figment of my young imagination and I'm hoping you can fill in the blanks. I'm not sure what happened to me so long ago," he explained in chopped breath, still reeling from his realization.

"Well, it's a lot to take in, but I think I can help in more than a few ways. Would it be alright if I come back tomorrow and show you my grandmother's account with her video interview that I recorded before coming here? I would then like to share the information I've unearthed?"

"Absolutely. Give me some time to tell my wife and get her caught up. Then she'll know what I know. She's my best friend."

"I assumed as much. Until tomorrow then."

Amelia was emotionally exhausted by her find and knew her excitement would not allow rest or sleep find her easily that evening.

When Amelia returned the next day, her greeting was far more welcoming. As she entered the large family room, to her surprise, the Woods' adult children were there.

Bart stood up and began addressing the group. "Thanks for coming, kids. I've been long keeping a secret from you and I think I can share it now and explain with this young lady's help. I've never known where I was from, well not really," Bart paused, "Are you getting this young lady?"

Amelia had already begun recording and smiled gratefully as just knowing Bart,(Sam) was alive would give her grandmother such relief. What a gift. In filming the event, Amelia became part of the mystery and a powerful force, healing a blemished, tumultuous history.

"I came to Canada when I was a child with a program that was called the British Home Boys program. There were a lot of us orphans who were sent to Canada, even Australia to work on farms, get adopted. I was one of the lucky ones. Not all of us were met with a family like mine. For some, it went very badly. The Woods family took me in, raised me as one of their own, loved me as their son and adopted me. I've had a very happy life from that point on and am very blessed. Just looking at you now, I feel terrible to have kept this secret from my past. It's tough to grow up believing you have been given away or worse, thought of as human trash and thrown away. I was humiliated, embarrassed and I'm sorry.

I know I shipped out of London, England. That is all I know. I was seven or eight but, the doctors weren't sure and I couldn't help them. See, I didn't know who I was. They found me wondering around in a field mumbling only two words, B and Algie. They named me Ben Algeirs and sent me on my way. It was worth money to them, finding boys to ship as Canadians paid to sponsor. It was a business. When I arrived here, I couldn't speak and Ma

Woods, she loved me well and in a year, I was reading and writing like the rest of the Woods family and I never turned back. They named me Bartholomew after my father, Mr. Woods, when I was adopted. I was their only son and suddenly I had a family and three sisters. That's my story except that I would sometimes dream of a young woman named B and boy named Algie.

Then yesterday, this young lady showed up and set my heart alive when I saw her face. I remembered I had a Nanny and her name was Nanny B. When found in the field, I had only two things, this old carpet bag and these three keys on a chain. One key was held in my hand so hard, it took days for me to let it go. That's why my hand cramps so much in the cold. I keep a key close by and hold it in my hand in case I need to defend myself and I've taught you all to do the same. I don't know why I have always done this or feel so strongly about it and today, together, I'm hoping Amelia can explain the missing pieces."

As Bart sat down, Amelia noticed how his wife had sympathetic tears in her eyes. Amelia stood and began the difficult, necessary and momentous explanation.

"I am here to solve a mystery for my grandmother, affectionately referred to as Nanny Beatrice Freeman. I am her granddaughter and she has suffered for many years amidst a scandal. What will matter to her most is not the scandal, but to know her charge, the young, Master Samuel Beckwith, lived. I took video of my grandmother's account. She is still in England and has never moved from her house until recently when she was forced to be placed in hospital. She is 85 years old and still cries at the thought of the lost little boy she loves. She refused to even consider moving or selling her house in the event the little boy found himself wondering in her neighbourhood in the hope he could remember her taking him there for tea with her own mother. She has held out hope all these years even amidst being thought of as a murderer, and worse.

Bart and his family watched and listened to Beatrice's account. They cried with compassion imagining the surreal history of little Sam Beckwith, who became Ben Algiers and finally Bart Woods. Bart, his wife and their son, James, decided they would return to England with Amelia to put B's mind at ease and to hopefully help to solve a mystery, find family and right wrongs.

Their first stop to test their theory was to check the keys that Bart held dear all these years. They went with Amelia to her grandmother's house and the first key did not fit the latch, nor did the second, but the third, fit and opened the door. Bart said later that moment drew shivers. One key was to the Beckwith house, one was to Beatrice's neighbour's house in case of emergency and one was to her own family home where she and the children had visited many times on outings. Amelia said her grandmother always hoped that if Sam had her keys, he knew the way to her house and might find her one day and so she could never move. Bart went in and stared to cry. "I've had warm milk and biscuits in this house! I know the smell of this house. It's like coming home." Bart's memories began to trickle into consciousness.

As emotional as it was, more difficult was to visit Scotland Yard and reveal what Amelia had uncovered. The cold case investigators were astounded, assuring Amelia she had encountered very good luck finding Bart, noting her journey could have turned out very differently. That aside, investigators then took the bag and keys to run tests. The test on the keys proved positive for blood that matched Bart, (Sam's family) and they found a second match and a third. That match would make investigators gasp for what the findings would imply. Nothing could be stated publicly until absolutely verified. It was decided that Bart wouldn't meet with Beatrice until the whole story was known and it didn't take long.

Two short days later, a group of men in their late sixties, those who were still alive from that long ago, two night outing on a train, gathered. They gathered and cried together at Scotland Yard, overwhelmed to just be standing in each other's presence. Still not speaking directly about what was unfolding or what had occurred, Amelia was keen to observe the men's reactions. Finally an Inspector entered the room.

"Gentleman, you have long been amidst a scandalous mystery from your childhood that can now be laid to rest with the help and luck from this young woman, Amelia Freeman. Amelia is the granddaughter of one of the long-time suspected accomplices, in the suspected murder of Samuel Beckwith, a then Miss Beatrice Freeman. As you know, Scotland Yard had arrested the school Head Master, Mr. Henry Jones for the suspected death of young Master Sam Beckwith and the tampering with children who attended the overnight on a train. It now appears we've had the wrong man."

The room remained silent. The men did not turn and look to each other in astonishment and there were no gasps of surprise to be heard. Amelia found this reaction curious. She looked at them one by one, sitting beside each other in a row and could imagine them as they were so long ago, boys, children, terrified, side by each in their own tormented club of powerless victims, and speechless in their shame, guilt and fear.

"Forensics now reveals a blood connection to the Head Master's assistant, Mr. Wenton, of whom I am certain you are all familiar with."

The room remained silent as the inspector continued.

"It was with the verified return of Samuel Beckwith that we were able to conclude the trace blood samples found on the keys and carpet bag in Beckwith's possession, were that of three different people, Samuel Beckwith in the bag, Mr. Wenton on the keys, and the third sample on the outside of the carpet bag, that of a Thomas Musgrave. Thomas as you may remember is a boy who also attended the train excursion, and is one of the twelve of you, but with one exception, Thomas unfortunately passed away a few years back. There's more on that score but first, Mr. Wenton…" the Inspector paused almost in disbelief.

"That brings us to the uncomfortable interview with now arrested Mr. Wenton who is well into his eighties. For your intended healing purposes, we will now play the interview with Mr. Wenton."

The former school boys and Amelia sat so very still as the suspense began to build in anticipation. Amelia wondered about the type of man Wenton truly was and was very curious to know if he lived with regret over what he had done, or if he even understood what he had done to the lives of these boys and all of their families. The interview began with Wenton sitting calmly, casually crossed legged, reclined, one arm over the back of the chair.

"Please state your name for our records?" the Inspector began questioning.

"I am Aaron Wenton, former Head Master of London's West Chester School For Boys."

"Do you recall a train ride over fifty years ago, the first of its kind under the direction of then Head Master Jones while you were his assistant, where twelve boys attended a two night school trip?"

"Oh yes, the best time. All the boys really enjoyed themselves," answered the now feeble looking old man, even paler than he once was and he seemed to enjoy himself at the attention he was getting. He sat back, repositioning still slouched, cross legged, relaxed, with one arm hanging over the back of interrogation chair.

"Do you confess to having engaged in sexual relations with all the boys on that trip?"

"Certainly not!"

"Do you care to clarify your response? Can you give us your version of the events?" the Inspector was insistent.

Very calmly and matter of factly, Wenton began, "One boy was never seen again! Put up a terrible fight, you know. Cut my hands, kicked and screamed. He was the only one to protest so vehemently! I was beginning to think he didn't want a grade at all! The others were game enough once I threatened to kill their families, but not this one. I think he died. Have you found Jones' carpet bag then?"

This portion of the interview did the trick. Tears fell and gasps were heard as disbelief in understanding took hold of the room. Wenton did not exhibit an ounce of remorse, but instead, pride!

"Can you explain the events of the last evening spent on the train?"

"Certainly, my pleasure. We finished tea and had our last evening sessions scheduled to review the boys' essays. I remember it like was yesterday. Jones and I swapped groups in order to share each group's work, Jones in his private room and me in the dining car. It was all very exciting. The boys were very talented, highly intelligent. I was drawing near the end of my list and instructed the boys to go to my room, one by one of course, to await their grade."

"Is that how and when you assaulted them?"

"Of course not! I graded them in my room! Assault is an ugly word. I wouldn't have bothered to grade you when you were a child. Unattractive little sot you must have been. Any teacher worth his salt would have done the same as I did. How would you expect me to honestly give the young boys a passing grade if I hadn't truly sampled them?"

"But something thwarted your plans?" the Inspector carried on.

"That damn, Jones! He finished up early and sent his group back to their God Forsaken Nannies! I was finished with that group the night before. The one boy, Algie, wasn't feeling well and needed a doctor. I didn't give him a very good grade. He passed of course, but he was not very, impressive. Algie was almost the least talented of the eleven I graded," Wenton paused, eyes drifting off into the distance, fondly remembering, then continued expressing frustration over Sam Beckwith.

"The boy, Sam, snuck off to his Nanny before I could grade him. He was scheduled for around nine p.m. I never warmed to his Nanny. Nanny Beatrice was her name, I believe. She had formed an unnatural attachment to the boy and was always staring at me, looking me in the eye, refusing to shake my hand, suspicious of me, which was very unbecoming and most notably, a disrespectful display exhibited from one in her decidedly base position in life."

"We know from passed interviews that Nanny Beatrice reported that you had come to Nanny Nancy's room to check on Algie, discovered she and Sam were in the room, offered your help, then you were hit on the head before she herself was attacked. Is this how you remember it?"

"Again with that damn blasted Nanny's account of ridiculousness! Yes I did come to the room but not to check on Algie! See, I already had given him a grade! I do wish you would pay attention. It's all very tiring, not to mention frustrating. Please try to follow. I had gone in search of Sam and knew the two boys were thick as thieves and surmised there was a possibility he had gone to Algie's sleeper car. I went to see if Sam was there and he was. As I turned to leave, that damn Jones was on his way to my car to get his carpet bag so we could begin the arduous task of packing up all the school supplies and such. I grabbed the hose from the wall and struck him on the head with the brass nozzle, knocking him to the floor. He hadn't seen me hit him, it was very convenient. I was resolved to complete my grading at any cost and Jones, that bumbling idiot was not going to get in my way."

"Yes, very well, what happened next?"

"That was when that frumpy, dim-witted Nanny Beatrice poked her head round the corner, so I hit her in the head with the hose head nozzle, took hold of Sam and proceeded to my car. It was Jones the Nanny saw on the floor, not me! Such a twit! However, she was conveniently incorrect on my behalf when all your colleagues were fumbling about asking all the wrong questions back then."

"What happened on the way to your car and what happened when you arrived at your car?"

"Well, I'm disappointed to tell you that I didn't get to grade the boy. I had placed him last on my list with high expectations."

"So sorry to hear that, please continue."

"Thank you for offering at least some empathy and I must say, you haven't been very kind during this interview!" Wenton repositioned himself, waved his hand in a continuing motion and expressed a very deep sigh of disappointment, rolling his eyes in an upward, disapproving motion before explaining further.

"Sam struggled, fought. He cut my hands, my neck, and just look at this scar above my brow! I wasn't certain I was up for it, but I'm not one to stray from a challenge."

"Please, carry on."

"Well, as you can imagine, I was bloodied by the time I arrived at my car. It was latch keys you know. Can't imagine where he got them from, probably that imbecilic Nanny of his. I would have preferred to have not banged Sam's head against the wall, but he made such a fuss!"

"You banged Sam's head against the wall? Which wall? The wall of hallway or were you already in the room?"

"I had managed to carry Sam into the room kicking and trying to scream. He wasn't cooperative, which was disappointing, you know how it is… When grading, it's preferred the boys are awake, but one can't have everything turn out well all of the time. I was just about to begin the grading process when the doctor knocked on my door, so I had to bang Sam's head against the wall a second time, knocking him unconscious because he would not be silenced! So, taking count, I banged his head twice against the wall in my room. I quickly stuffed him into the carpet bag, answered the door and when the doctor realized I had been attacked, he immediately ushered me to the dining car for treatment, where he had set up a station of sorts. And there you have it."

"So just to be clear, you graded eleven boys from your list?"

"Correct."

"Do you still have your list?' The Inspector
knew how psychopaths kept trophies and
mementos and gave the question a try never
expecting a response like the one he received.

"Of course!" And to the room's absolute
astonishment, Wenton produced an old piece of
paper from his vest coat that was folded very
small.

"Do you have any knowledge of what happened
to Mr. Jones' carpet bag?" asked the Inspector.

"I've never seen it again. It was not there when I
returned to my room and I cannot begin to
explain my disappointment and confusion. Do
you know?" Wenton asked coyly.

"Just to be clear, Mr. Wenton, are you actually
saying you placed Sam Beckwith unconscious,
bloodied, in Mr. Jones' carpet bag?"

"Yes! What else could be done? I thought I
would return afterwards to grade the boy but
when I returned the bag was gone and no sign of
the boy!"

"It never occurred to you to confess?"

"Confess to what? Why would I do that?"

"Certainly investigators questioned you?"

"Ah, but they never did ask the right questions, so no- no I didn't feel like offering information, especially as I had done nothing wrong. Jones was the "Head Master" and he wanted to take responsibility."

"Nothing, wrong?! " the Inspector asked incredulously.

"No Sir! The boys were very talented and co-operative."

"Are you aware that Algie killed himself not days after upon hearing you had become the Head Master of the School? The eight year old boy hung himself!"

"I told you he was not as talented as the other boys! I told you he was disappointing," Wenton responded, frustrated at the Inspector's lack of understanding Algie's obvious deficiencies.

"And again, just to be clear. There was a boy who was lost on the train for over forty minutes, a Thomas Musgrave?"

"Is there a question, Inspector?" Wenton smiled out of the side of his mouth.

"Did you know the whereabouts of Thomas during the time when you say you were with the doctor in the dining car?"

"No sir! I did not know his whereabouts, but I can tell you he was impressive, got a very good grade," Wenton smirked in memory of his conquest and winked at the inspector.

"You Sir represent all that is wrong with humanity. I will wear your not being captured as a smear on the excellent reputation of Scotland Yard. I am sorry we couldn't have caught you earlier. You have scorched the lives of so many. You do not deserve to live. I can only wonder what you have done in the time since that horrible train pilot project."

"Is that a question?"

"I beg your pardon?"

"Is that a question? Oh my dear Inspector, I've graded so many boys, repeatedly in fact." Wenton's proud smile obviously shocked the Inspector.

"What?!"

"And as I'm tired, I'm old, and won't be around for much longer, I have to know, did you find Jones' carpet bag?"

"Yes, yes we did in fact."

"Was young beautiful Sam in that bag?"
Wenton's demeanour changed, alert and smug,
he repositioned himself again, but this time he
leaned towards the Inspector in excitement over
his anticipation of the answer to the question.

"At one point, yes, yes he was."

Delight filled Wenton's face and he cunningly
smiled as though he were re-imagining the
possibility of reliving the experience in his
youth, as though Sam were still that eight year
old boy in need of grading and Wenton seemed
lost in a dear fantasy, where the outcome could
result in his favour, in his plan working out.

"For the record, do you have any regrets? We
will share this interview with the families
hoping to give them closure and help them with
a feeling of healing."

"Oh, I see, my message to the families,"
Wenton paused contemplatively, still smiling,
mentally reminiscing in his reverie before
continuing.

"Oh, I now see what you are feeling. Allow me
to explain. I am not responsible for what you or
anyone else is 'feeling'!" Sarcasm and mockery
billowed from Wenton. "With respect, your
'feelings' are very much your own and have

nothing to do with me, therefore I am not 'sorry' for how you or anyone else may 'feel.' If you or anyone has 'hurt' feelings, then you are responsible to keep your feelings in check, not me. At this very moment, you put me in mind of that horrid Nanny Beatrice actually, looking at me, judging me with your inferior intelligence and lack of wit. I think you are becoming fond of me. I am a fisherman, Inspector, did you know?"

"No, I was unaware of that fact." The Inspector began packing up his paperwork.

"My fishing partner and I have sat up late many nights. He talked Perch and Salmon and I always agreed with his regret, you know, the one that got away?"

"Sam was the one that got away, like a fish and you're the fisherman?" the inspector asked incredulously.

"Look at my hands? Scarred with bitter remembrance, you see. Of course he was the one that got away. He was to be my crescendo, my piece de resistance!" Finally Wenton expressed regret however displaced.

"You Sir, and I use the term loosely, can go to your grave never knowing how Sam escaped you and you sir, cannot go back in time so take that smug look off your face before I slap it off!"

"You seem to exhibit violent tendencies, Inspector, delightfully surprising, I assure you," Wenton smiled excitedly, slyly, as he ran his tongue along his top teeth and top lip with every ounce of warped interest in provoking the Inspector while expressing his attraction to such behaviour.

"Sam Beckwith will never be graded by you! You are a piece of dirt and a scourge on society! Get him out of here!" The Inspector shouted the order expressing his disgust, horror and personal outrage towards such a psychopath and pedophile.

The room was silent but for the tears the men shed. Even though Sam had been returned to them by some miracle, the sadness, grief, and shock they endured would never part from them. As Amelia looked around the room she took notice of the men and imagined them again as frightened little boys with their heads down in a secret brotherhood especially as they had all thought Wenton had killed Sam. What recourse did they have then? Surely they, as mere boys were all certain that Wenton could and would kill their families as he had threatened.

The Inspector, saddened by this, pressed his lips together and addressed the men.

"I know this has been very hard. In addition to Sam fighting Wenton off, there is another youngster we must mention. His name is Thomas and many of you remained in school with him. He carried a secret with him the whole course of his life, one that nearly destroyed him. He never married, never had children and could never forgive himself."

"Forgive himself?" questioned one of the men, wiping away his tears.

"He left a letter in his will. I think it will make sense now and is possibly the last piece of the puzzle. He requested this letter be added to the case file upon his death, but only if there were inquiries to the case. His solicitor brought it in upon request by Scotland Yard. Gentlemen, steel yourselves."

And the Inspector began to read.
"I am Thomas. I was 8 years old when a monster took my life from me while on that damn train. I was Wenton's number 11. I was told to return to my nanny when Wenton left me

in his sleeper car, ravaged, devastated, in pain, my nose bleeding from being struck, but found I couldn't move. I couldn't think straight. Fear must have gripped my mind. There's something horrible that happens to a youngster when a monster steals your life, takes your soul. I was still in shock when Wenton returned to his room and I hid in the drapery, barely breathing. I watched Wenton bang Sam's head into the wall and shove'm in the bag. Then, the doctor came for Wenton. Damn straight I grabbed that bag! I dragged it to the next car exit and threw it off the train! I'd be damned to let something worse happen to Sam than what had just happened to me, happen to one of my own. We were all mates, you must understand. We, none of us knew if we'd get out of there alive. I believed Wenton when he said he'd kill my family and I did not fight. I saw what Sam had done. He fought. He tried to defend himself. I saw the scratches.

Sam was brave. So I made my mind up. I could fight too. One of us was going to make it out alive. I thought of jumping off too, but fear gripped me and I just sat crying for the longest time, until they found me. Mine is a life of sadness, shame and regret. I never thought for a moment I would have killed Sam like they all said happened to him. May God Forgive me, and Sam too, even if he keeps with Angels up in heaven. I hope mate, you can forgive me too.

Sincerely and regretfully yours, Thomas."

The Inspector took a deep breath and paused before continuing.

"Thomas died never knowing Sam actually lived, just like all of you here today. As you now know Sam's story, there was no record of him and we suspect he was in shock, and more than likely suffering a concussion, fortunate to be alive after Wenton's brutal attack. Upon other interviews, Wenton did confess to hoping to kill Sam, not just 'grade him'. It's unclear what happened to Thomas exactly, but Wenton had escalated in his brutality as he graded you boys. This is the list Wenton proudly provided."

A copy of the paper was passed round the room. The men read the list of their names, Algie being number six, Thomas, number eleven, and Sam number twelve, the big fish, the one that got away.

"Thomas didn't feel he had time to check in the bag, he just needed to save his school mate. He did what he thought was right. You know the rest," the Inspector paused turning to Bart

(Sam), "When you couldn't be found, he must have felt responsible for your death."

The Inspector's face had reddened from the stress of the overwhelming emotion that filled the room.

"Back then, you boys went to the funeral of Beckwith, assuming Jones had killed him. So Thomas, just eight years old, in addition to his horrific experience with Wenton, lived with the thought he had killed you, Sam, when in fact, he had in all likeliness, saved your life. After all these years, it's a bitter sweet reunion gentleman. It's absolutely remarkable."

Amelia wiped tears from her eyes. Bart sat shocked as even more memories returned. The Inspector then turned to Bart and said, "We still have a few loose ends to tie up."

The Inspector raised his arm and ushered for people to enter the room.

The men all stood as Bart(Sam) was reunited with his sister and his mother, now almost 92 years old, confined to a wheel chair. His father had passed away but his mother held him like life had returned. The men wept with joy at the reunion as a bit of humanity had been returned to them in that moment, assuring them there is still good in the world.

Bart introduced Amelia and Bart's mother asked to accompany them to the Nursing home where Beatrice was about to get the shock of her life.

"Nan?" Amelia poked her head around the door of the hospital room.

"Yes, Amelia, yes, dear! Oh I am so pleased you are back! How I have missed you!"

Not being able to find the words for the introduction, Bart simply entered the room and Sam was returned to Nanny B, a moment frozen in time and torment erased as her young charge was returned to her. Tears streamed down Beatrice's face, "Oh my dear!" Beatrice gasped with joy recognizing her young charge immediately. "I knew you lived! I knew you must be out in the world. Oh how I've prayed for you and just look at you!"

As Bart slowly walked towards her, Beatrice saw her young Master Sam and with each step he aged into the man who stood before her. He sat down on the bed beside his beloved Nanny B, leaned in and gave the now old woman a big hug. He breathed her in, and she smelled the same, lavender and rose and he could barely contain himself. They broke their embrace and sat staring into each other's eyes. Beatrice held his face in her hands and through her tears, she smiled. "My word, Master Sam, does no one take after you now?" she asked as she brushed his curls down with her hand. Bart's wife chuckled into her hand at the sweet reunion and could imagine Beatrice putting Bart's hair right before he went to school. Bart smiled in fond remembrance of his dear caretaker who he loved so much.

Bart's mother was wheeled over to Beatrice and held out her hand. "I am so sorry Nanny Beatrice. It was such a difficult time. We didn't know what to think."

"Our beautiful boy is back! That's all that ever mattered to me." Beatrice answered without bitterness, without meanness, it just wasn't in B's nature to be cruel.

"I think you should have these, B. Thank you. You helped save my life all those years ago."

"My word! I wondered if you had them. I couldn't even get into my own house when the time came! Had to have them re-made. I never left, you know. Just in case you might have wandered over. I never left, well, until now needing care and such, but I never sold the place, never changed the locks, even kept my family name in case you needed to find me," Beatrice smiled proudly in the wisdom of her resolve.

A teary eyed Amelia stood leaning her shoulder on the door of the hospital room, arms folded, "My work here is done," she whispered to herself.

For the young filmmaker however, her work was just beginning as Wenton's story would take years to fully uncover, expose and became one of the widest pedophilia rings uncovered in British history reaching Amsterdam, Belgium, Spain, Portugal, Russia, Australia, United States and Canada.

The entire story now unfolded, Amelia Freeman, researcher, crime stopper, film maker, would come to realize a simple truth. Love is a powerful thing, hope can save lives, and in stories such as these, heroes can be born, hearts can be mended, time can heal wounds, criminals can get punished, and most of all one must always remember to keep latch keys close at hand in case of encountering pirates and monsters.

Monsters as we well know come in all shapes and sizes and can hide in plain sight just about anywhere.

The End

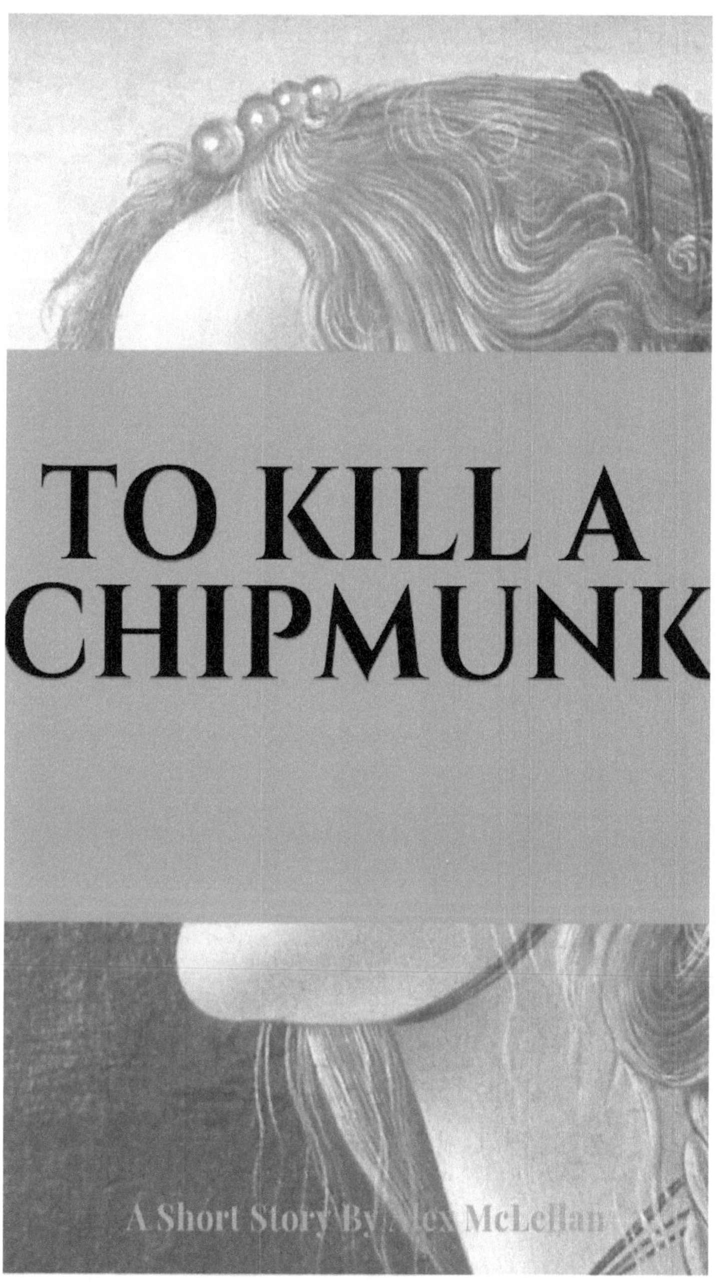

TO KILL A CHIPMUNK

I dedicate this story to my lifelong, dear friend, Susan. The world, and especially my world is a better place because you are in it and your light shines so bright.

Thank you, Susan.

To Kill A Chipmunk

I lay in a hospital bed, completely mindful, aware yet somehow, suspended, barely breathing, and barely alive. I could tell that death was very near. In my dreamy reverie, I contemplated life and death. I suppose most take this opportunity once resigned to their fate.

I closed my eyes and allowed a meditative sleep to overcome me. Only the sound of the respirator that kept me breathing could be heard. Occasionally, I would hear voices, sometimes crying, others wishing me well, others confessing what they felt they should have confessed years ago, and my favourite, those voices who whispered their permission for me to just, 'let go'. How arrogant does a person have to be to give me 'permission' to do anything. If I could have slapped them, I would have. They didn't interrupt me, I dreamed on.

I dreamed of important incidents in my life. I dreamed of shocking, embarrassing, hysterical, treasured memories. How vividly they visited me, and how quickly they left me. I could not touch them, or relive them. I could only watch, witnessing my life reflectively, emotionally embracing all of my experiences.

At one point, I remembered my best friend Susan's face at her grandfather's funeral. Such expression of profound loss the likes I had not seen before. Such emptiness embedded with misunderstanding in her eyes. "He's gone now," I remember her saying with tearful eyes.

That memory made me wonder what my own funeral would be like. Preparations would have likely already begun, I reckoned. I remembered another time when Susan and I were teenagers. We had been walking in the woods and we noticed a dying chipmunk by roadside. It suffered tremendously making horrible, painful wailing and crying sounds. I turned my head as Susan crushed the chipmunk with a large rock.

"It was for the best," she said sadly.

"I know I'd be grateful if I were the chipmunk," I answered honestly.

Then suddenly, for some reason following that memory, I wanted to do everything over again. I wanted to re-marry my husband, have another child, another house, car, earrings, new perfume, but alas time was not my friend and I knew it was the imaginings of a dying woman.

Following the chipmunk incident, I remembered copying these words, words I believed then, words I believed now.

'Being of sound mind and body, I hereby command my family and friends and medical staff to heed my wishes. Should I be rendered invalid of any of my personal capabilities and can no longer function independently, or am unable to return to my life as I now know and enjoy it, I wish to be removed from all life support endeavours of any kind. I will not be maintained, I do not wish to be a burden financially, emotionally, or otherwise. I believe that no one I love will be able to live knowing I am only existing, strapped to wires, unable to further my life and I ask everyone to remember, it is my life."

I recalled the words as though raindrops softly fell against my face. I realized things I wanted to do now, I had already done, already enjoyed, already lived. I hoped they understood that it wasn't that I wanted to go, it was simply that I couldn't stay. For the first time, I had to convince myself to go forward, to push on. Perhaps I would experience the most interesting adventure of my life…death.

While I lay there, I could feel a tear form in my eyes then gently, slowly make its way down my cheek. It was Susan's voice I heard now as my best friend visited me.

"I don't know if you can hear me," she spoke softly, "I won't leave you like this. I love you too much to selfishly keep you lingering on like this, especially knowing what you want to happen."

I loved her dearly. We'd known each other for most of our lives. We could tell each other anything and everything and know that we accepted each other, cherished our friendship, sharing an empathic bond of sisterhood, knowing we were loved and have loved. With just a look, we could understand without speaking what was needed and that power, that ability to share our lives with confidence and trust is a blessing, an irreplaceable gift. I knew I could rely on her for anything and everything and here she was, supporting my every decision.

Footsteps poured in. I was aware of everyone as they gathered to bid me farewell. My youngest of five, late at birth and overdue now as well rushed in last, huffing and puffing.

"I found the letter. It's official now. I love you, Mom, we all do."

"Alright now," Susan spoke compassionately standing at my husband's side.

They each took hold of my hand and placed the cord in my palm, enclosing my limp fingers over it as they helped to support my hand. I could hear they were crying as Susan said, "We'll do this together. We love you so very much."

"I won't say good-bye because I love you madly and I will see you on the other side, my sweet love, my best friend," my husband wept.

And me, just about unable to speak a word. With the weight of my hand, the cord released from the respirator and I felt a strange gratitude and peace surround me as my last breath passed and the respirator was removed.

"Dad?" my daughter asked.

"Yes, I heard it too."

"What did she say?"

"Thank you."

The End

Nee

A Short Story By Alex McLellan

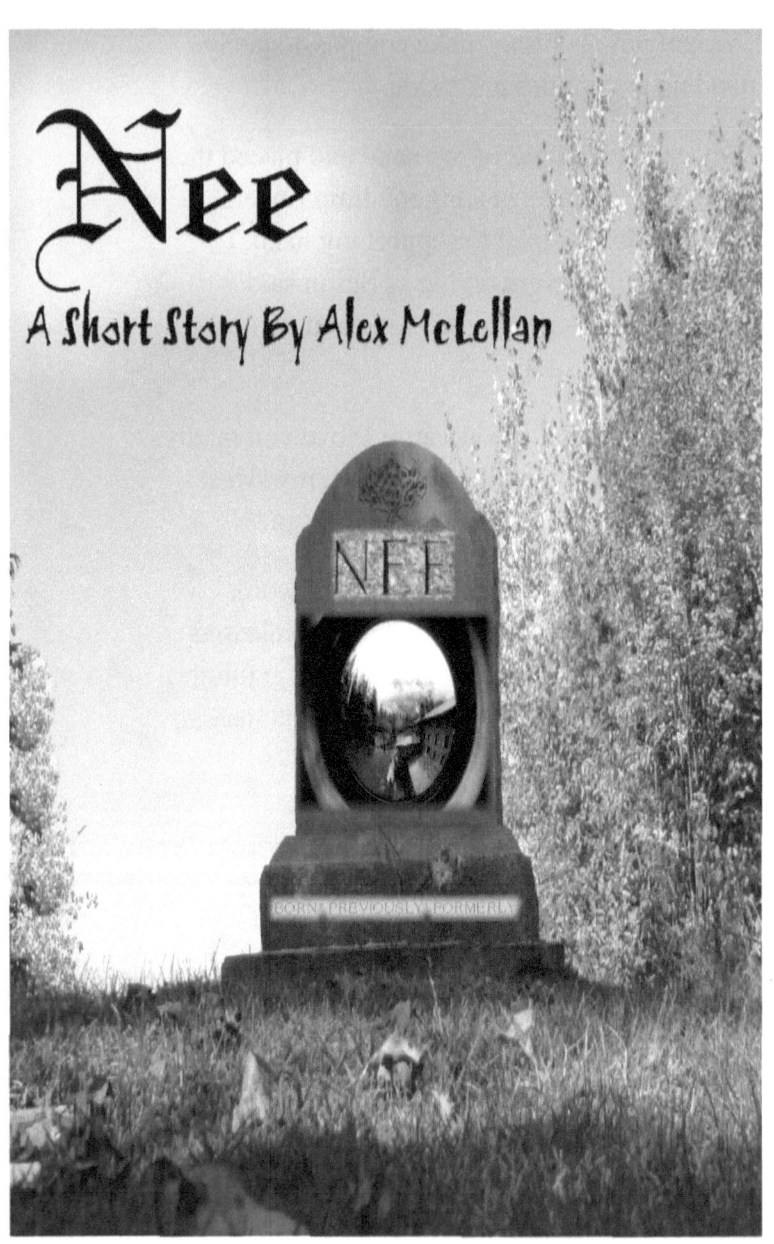

Author's Note:

Nee is a particular story most unlike the
previous stories in this collection of shorts.

Nee adopts a unique style of writing which
embraces the elongated sentence structure
favoured by writers in history.

Nee is my gift to readers who enjoy stretching
the imagination, probing age old questions and
do not mind contemplating the unthinkable.

Alex McLellan

Nee

What began as a suspicion soon became an obsession, a deep seeded desire to understand the unknown, the apparent coincidental incident, and the overwhelming pre-occupation to comprehend information the eyes did see, but the mind could not fathom.

Every now and then, this wonderful life produces an anomaly, an exception to the rule, a new en-heightened awareness. In order to truly appreciate the unusualness of this particular tale, one must understand there is no evidence to prove the contrary, perhaps the most frightening and uncomfortable aspect of our tale. One may choose not to believe. One may choose to suppose the entire concept a farce. One may choose to realize, of all the controversies ever known to man, one indisputable fact stands true above all religious doctrine, all political viewpoints, and every philosophy, theosophy, theology:

Man lives and man dies.

What occurs in between these two instances is any man's guess, really.

Whether we choose to agree or disagree on the very distinct matter of what in fact actually is the beginning or the ending of our lives, for our purposes, I will begin this tale at a beginning or sorts, which may prove to result in a new desirous obsession of your own, dear reader, an insatiable, possibly personally destructive urge to know for certain. Your mind will open and your quest for true understanding will begin.

Only one question will remain however.

Are you prepared to accept the answers you will find?

Nee
Adjective: born, previously, formerly

History

There is a very famous photograph taken in 1966 by Reverend R.W Hardy while visiting the Queen's House in Greenwich, England.
While visiting with his wife, the tourist was enthralled with the famous Tulip Staircase, so enthralled, he captured the memory on film.
Upon returning home and having the film developed, a ghostly image was discovered appearing to be running up the staircase.
It is indisputably unexplainable and said to be an authentic account of the paranormal caught on film. There are still to this very day, live accounts of footsteps heard, a seemingly transparent woman walking through walls, and yet another transparent young lady at the foot of the stairs mopping up what appears to be blood.
Rumour has it that a young chamber maid met an untimely violent death having been thrown from the top of the famous Tulip Staircase.
This photograph can be found at https://imgur.com/a/lurvjrp

The Tulip Staircase Ghost Photo

Let Us Begin…

I can reveal to you the capture of this apparition
for all the world to see was a stroke of luck for
the photographer, a mistake in nature of colossal
proportion and an unlikely moment which began
a sequence of events bringing us to this very
story.
There are many instances and beginnings which
correspond to the very date the ghost
photograph was captured, and the birth of a little
girl is one such instance, a very, shall we say,
different sort of child.

Yes indeed, a series of events would ensue and
we must take the opportunity to point out that
this particular child was born in 1966 at the very
moment the photograph was taken.

One evening when the child was three years old,
she and her family prepared to attend a Drive-In
theatre. They lived in a second floor apartment.
As the family prepared to exit, the child, who
wore a long nightgown, held her pillow in front
of her as she took her first step down the stairs.

For those of you unfamiliar with the wearing of
nightgowns, the next revelation may well be a
surprise to you. Nevertheless, tripping on the
front of her nightgown, down the flight of stairs
the three year old went, producing a crying

child, a nose bleed and three very bad bumps on the head. Of course, the family went to the Drive-In and life continued.

Although a little leery of stairs in general, the child had survived the first encounter, the first clue, and it was this incident that we mark as a beginning, and an ending.

This child was exceptionally different from other children. Her dreams were especially vivid, and on occasion, she reported to her mother or to anyone who would listen, that she had seen certain things. However, a little girl from the small town in Kirkland Lake, Ontario, Canada, where she was from, couldn't have ever known of Indian carpets, the lady in white who runs up and down the flower stairs, (which we may refer to properly as the Tulip staircase), complained of hearing whispers, reported seeing artwork on rounded ceilings, and the 'what if' questions she produced that often later occurred.

The oddities about this child often spooked those around her including her own mother.

Even the child herself began to wonder about her "other" family, the other places she lived and other people she may have known, "before" she was this version of -herself. That very concept was life altering. She was becoming aware. Her subconscious was becoming awakened and slowly life would change for her in very big ways.

Time did pass and as many lives seem to follow down a frightening path, so did the now young woman's.

Her life however was complicated and she began to dream of other lives, other loves and when sleep found her, she felt more alive than when she was quite awake.

Eventually, there came an awful day for the now mother of two. Her husband, a foul minded individual decided to help her with the arduous task of walking down a flight of stairs by saving her time, providing her with the gentle push she needed to break her neck in the fall. With the experience seemingly ending there, she lay quite dead at the bottom on the landing. A definite ending some might say.

Ah, but beginnings and endings are confusing, intermingled things combined with time which few can measure or understand.

In short, not realizing what had happened, the young mother, so dedicated to survival and the mothering of her children, rose slowly until she was standing. She looked up to her husband who immediately rushed down the stairs to see if she was actually alright and asked her how it happened that she had fallen. The unsettling experience brought to mind her fall down a flight of stairs as a child, and left a very strange, dark, frightening feeling that stuck with her as she had recalled wondering if her own mother had pushed her down the stairs in a hurry to attend the Drive-In movie.

Dazed and confused, the couple decided the incident had been the weirdest of things and life continued. Of course, the marriage did not. The divorced young mother of two carried on with the children. Several sad and exhausting years would pass.

While driving one day, the woman's mind began to wander. She looked off into the distance and realized the geography had changed somehow. There were two very large houses that she had never noticed before. While the road seemed not to have altered, the land around it seemed to have grown in and around fences in a most unfamiliar way, overgrown as though twenty years had passed since the day before. Since this was a road she travelled every day, these thoughts and observations struck her very oddly. She became fearful, anxious and she whispered out loud,

"I wonder if I did die when I fell down the stairs and all of this, all of everything is just me fabricating a life, when my old life stopped and I didn't?"

Shivers ran over her and she drove a little slower while the sky seemed impossible colors and the clouds looked like a child painted them on.

"If I died and I carried on, then the old me, could be in a coma somewhere, while I am here. How do I get back? Do I even want to go back? I mean the kids are safe with me here. What about my kids? I wonder if versions of them are still in harm, there? But is here real? Or is there real? I'm being silly. It's the strangest thought. It can't be real, but I can't shake it."

She picked up her now teenage son from his part time job and tried very hard not think of it again.

But dreams they say are communications with the soul, and her dreams were especially relentless. Suddenly she could remember different versions of her many selves. She remembered being a version who suffered amnesia. She remembered being another version who had married a cowboy. She remembered being a peasant woman, a mother of four, and she could see the children's faces as she lay dying, leaving them to their own devices. Death was after all, not a planned thing.

Every morning she awoke feeling just a little like she had not left her dream state entirely behind and eventually began to wonder other thoughts.

"What if there are many versions of me kicking around? What then? Who am I really? What if I died when my ex-husband pushed me down the stairs? Am I dead? Where do I belong? Do I get to choose? I must be crazy! If it were that easy, we'd all be doing it!"

But what our single mother of two didn't realize was she was actually not the only one having these thoughts, these concerns, these longings for answers to questions. He was there too. He was there in every version of herself in every moment she had ever lived and he hated her with a passion reserved for those who make dictionary definitions, creating new words describing new levels of hatred, passion, and the exaggerated not known until now.

She began to accept the concept of death in a new light. She, up to this point did not figure out how stair cases fit into it, but all would be revealed and soon.

She could feel he was near. In this life, he was her ex-husband. She had dodged a bullet twice.

In her past life, instead of passing away when he smothered her with a pillow, she existed simultaneously between the threads of fabric we refer to as time, and while in one dimension, her dead body lie in the bed, dressed in her favourite white sleeping attire, successfully murdered, she, her "self" ran for her life up the staircase where she had the misfortune of not even knowing she was being photographed. Thus, the legend of the White Lady and the Tulip Staircase began.

It has been said that energy cannot be created or destroyed, only transformed. The body is merely a casing, a shell, and this woman had escaped her shell many times over as others have done before her. And so the entire concept of ghostly encounters now explained may strike you as absurd. But alas, her time had come again. He had finally found her and this time he would finish her for good. Being a sociopath, he had developed an awareness of a kind and he, in the deep, dark, recesses of his criminal mind had resolved she was a witch of sorts and that suspicion made his task all the more an attractive challenge.

One night, before nine pm. on her way to pick up her son from his part time job, she realized she had forgotten her driver's license and returned home. In a hurry, she rushed into the house and immediately was struck with the feeling something was wrong. The wallet was not by the door, two of the lights had been turned off and though odd, not worth spending time investigating, making her son wait. She rushed into her bedroom and noticed the wallet on the bed. She thought it was strange and couldn't remember leaving it there. She reached for it and that is when she knew something was more than wrong. Finally after a day of rationalizing, blatantly disregarding and flat out ignoring, she listened closely to the little voice within and just knew... he was there!

She could sense that old feeling of dread and fear gripped her. She was certain he stood behind her. He had been hiding in the closet for hours, waiting. He had just walked right in, earlier in the day, while she was home and he waited. She stood paralyzed and suddenly could feel his breath at the back of her neck.

"I told you. Steal my children? Ruin my life? It's over for you, witch bitch!" And he reached over her neck and grabbed her chin, snapping her neck, dragging her out of the bedroom and throwing her down the stairs. And just like when he had pushed her down the flight of stairs while they were married, he stood convinced she had died, but on this occasion, something was different.

A cool breeze brushed by him. In her mind, she had once again ran for her life and it was after all, her mind, but he sensed her spirit and while he stared down at the dead mother of his two children, the psychopath became riddled with a paranoid fear of the unexplained. Remember, he had developed an awareness of a kind.

Suddenly, he felt the invisible, unexplainable impact from behind that would end his life, sending him down the flight of stairs. The last two things he would see on this earth was at first as he lay broken at the foot of the stairs, the dead body of the woman he had finally killed who lay open eyed, lifelessly at his side, and secondly, as movement caught his eye, he looked to the top of the stairs and in his amazement and practical disbelief, stood the victorious, transparent image of the woman he believed he had finally killed. A ghost? No! It was her! He hadn't really killed her. She was no witch, she was something else. So terrified, he died instantly, befittingly and to everyone's relief.

In order to explain how this is possible, one must backtrack to the beginning of our tale and realize life has lessons for us all. Once such lesson learned was captured on film as our heroin whom was mentioned first and rightfully so, escaped her shell and ran up and down a staircase and didn't stop running until she righted a wrong that had been done to her in that life.

Centuries later, she stopped running as fate, energy and precise circumstance brought her to the very person who had taken her life in their own lifetime. Yes indeed, he was the very man if we may presume to call him a man and not a monster who murdered his wife. Even though he told people he had awakened to find she had passed in her sleep, he was merely truthfully satisfying a deep desire to witness life flow from the living, believing he, himself had the power to have her life force absorbed into his own. He hadn't even fathomed the energy escaping, and continuing on in a relentless loop of experience relived, and the soul's adaptation, carrying on, continuing life. Her "ghostly" image ran and ran in a vicious cycle for centuries until the moment arrived when time and fate once again, like magnets brought the two energies together again in a fierce collision where time itself did bend.

The impact of the collision however, threw him physically down a flight of stairs, killing him almost instantly allowing her to move on, transform as her energy released itself from a secondary shell of the subconscious.

There will be no more photographs of the white lady running up or down the famous Tulip Staircase.

If only ghost hunters were astute, which they are not, they would invent some sort of device to capture those who walk about during the day. Why wait unit the night to seek revenge, right a wrong, move an item with invisible hands?

Haven't you, dear reader, felt the hair stand on the back of your neck when fear gripped you inexplicably? Do you not suppose someone may be actually at your side, waiting for the moment to right a wrong? How many times have we heard stories where people state, they don't know how they made it out alive, or they don't understand how they didn't die? Perhaps they did die and like our heroine, simply not knowing, they carried on in an alternate, more agreeable subconscious fabrication they never questioned was not reality.

In modern society, we hear of freak accidents where villainous people meet a very odd and shall we say karmic fate. Truth is, there is an equal and opposite reaction to every action.

In this tale, appropriate reaction to being murdered took centuries to come right, many staircases, and even though she had no idea she was reliving and re-dying for centuries running up and down the flight of stairs, at the moment her ex-husband, looked at transparent " her", the great exchange took place. Knowledge was passed and she then knew what happened to her, remembering the gruesome, cold murder she experienced and shock of betrayal from someone she held so dear. She began sensing and understanding just how long she had been living the loop of her death experience.

A deep sadness found her. For it was then she realized her life had been a lie and her children were motherless in several other lifetimes. Her own parents lost their first child when the child was just three years old, and never did attend a drive-in movie after that, yet all the while she had carried on with them, but only in her mind. Paramount in experience is the fact that in every life she lived, her ex-husband took her. In every life he hated. In the very least we must realize he may find her once again, reawaken an old detest, after all, hatred is evil consistently, if anything. But for now her cycle could begin afresh, a new baby, a new soul.

This entire preface merely is one soul's tale. One consciousness, and all because a devoted mother couldn't fathom a truth of being murdered and leaving her children behind, running up a staircase, and being photographed as a ghost so many years ago.

A photograph of a subconscious image and that is all, not a ghost! The mere instant capture of fantastic documentation of an electrical communication between subconscious, conscious and the once familiar physical, not a ghost!

And no, the houses were not there, as the young mother drove to pick up her son from work. There is no such person, or persons. This, all of this, was merely a version of a consciousness never satisfied, a fabrication of consciousness intermingled with other mass fabrications. As the "collision time" drew nearer, the fabrications weakened and on occasion cracks of other fabrications, even slices of reality, uncomfortably trickled into view. When instances such as these occur, one gets a creepy sensation for a reason they are unable to explain.

The people she knew, the places she had been, none of it ever happened, or did it? Some think they see our heroin's vehicle around nine p.m. on the road where she had seen the landscape change on the way to pick up her son and are very confused as the vehicle often disappears from view and I hear them say out loud, "What the hell? I'm sure there was a car there a moment ago. Maybe there's something wrong with me."

And just what might that be, exactly? What do you suppose could be wrong? Dead, perhaps? Haven't you yourself awaken in a panic, frantically shouting your dream had seemed so "real"? How real was it? Were you day dreaming, or did you leave, for just a bit?

After all, there is however another photograph, not so famous, in a suitcase, in a shed, belonging to a former landlady long since passed, and she fancied herself a photographer. If one looks very carefully, a white disturbance is seen from the top of the staircase to the bottom. It is the staircase of an apartment building in Kirkland Lake, Ontario, a tiny town where a small child lost her life falling down a flight of stairs while wearing a nightgown. Ghost photograph or just threads in the fabric of time overlapping at the exact moment the photo was taken?

And now, as I do not in fact actually live and breathe and yet I am, I can tell you as I visit this 'would be' aspiring author, borrow her fingers, borrow her mind, just to tell you this story, I tell you with certainty, there is more to know and I do know it!

As I share this tale, there will be more to come, more to fear, more unexplained, and since you may not have deduced as of yet, I and my "many-selves," exist in between a beginning and an end by your definition, I say again, there is more to know and I know it.

And as you live and breathe, though you may not know which one of you, you truly are, dangling fate between the neither here nor there, the subconscious battling the conscious, the dream state struggling to take over a person's idea of a waking state, I am with. I am within.

When you next visit a graveyard to pay your respects, whisper a prayer for a dear one who is in your mind, passed away and perhaps "feel" something curious, think you see a shadow out of the corner of your eye, think you may have felt a presence and denied my voice within, it all may be true in a manner of speaking.

Perhaps time is visiting you! Perhaps you are experiencing an awaking and realizing re-incarnation doesn't happen, but the sensation of the experience, in fact does exist in the way of familiarity. The next time someone tells you, you remind them of someone they once knew long ago who passed, perhaps your response should be, "Stranger things have happened." Could you be that person in another reality? Perhaps the next time you find yourself somewhere so familiar you find the need to explain it with Déjà vu, you will remember the other possibility I have presented, and ask your 'self', if perhaps your fabrications are weakening, crisscrossing, overlapping.

You may not know where your future lies, but I know it!

I do visit dream states from time to time, send messages, inspire, impersonate, confuse, elaborate and entertain my many "selves" and it was I who heard you ask questions when you thought you were talking to your "self".

But at this moment, as our great exchange may seemingly be coming to a close, I bring warning, whispered caution in the way of impending, foreboding thoughts of the macabre. Feeling a little, dead, perhaps?

Steal Yourself And Take Heed:

Should you feel fear,

You may think you see,

And if you are scared,

Be prepared,

I see you

For my name is

Nee.

Afraid of shadows in the night?

Heard a strange sound?

Caught a fright?

Do not fear only night this way,

Fear will now find you

In the light of day.

Oh, I'll be by,

In the corner of your eye,

In your mind,

You will find,

Quiet moments to recall...

Oh yes, I know it all.

We will meet when the time is right,

Rest assured, no need to fight,

For you already suspect too well,

Yours may be the next tale I tell!

Who or what am I you ask?

Who am I to take you to task?

Person, place, or thing, or not?

I am all time and you forgot..

It's quite alright to be afraid,

Especially of me,

Dead?

I have heard whispers,

You may already be…

Forget me not!

For I am all, and my name is...

Nee!

The End

Acknowledgements

*The cover for both The Mourning Window and In Light Of Ardith short stories are original photography taken by Alex McLellan at the beautiful and scenic location of Violet Hill, Ontario on Highway 89 where the wonderful Mrs. Mitchell's Restaurant, Granny Taught Us How and Heidi's Room is located. For more information about this location, contact Mrs. Mitchell's Restaurant at 519-925-3627 or info@mrsmitchells.com.

*Landscaping of these beautiful grounds by the Lesa Peat Gardener, an exceptional landscaping company.

*Covers for the book, created with the help of Canva and Kindle Direct Publishing. Covers for It Happened One Halloween Night, The Big Clouds, To Kill A Chipmunk, and The Doctor were created with the help of Canva which can be found online at https://www.canva.com/

*Layout, Editing, and posting on Amazon Kindle Publishing by Nathan Sher & Alex McLellan.

 **About the Author**

Author, Illustrator and Entrepreneur, Alex
McLellan, lives in Shelburne, Ontario, Canada
with her loving husband and beautiful co-
author, Miles the Cat.

"I write because I have to write. Writing
is a compulsion for me, an addiction, an
inexplicable power steeling the
imagination, creating a doorway into
another world where anything can
happen. Who if given a choice would not
choose to live in such a world?"

Alex McLellan

More works by Alex McLellan

can be found on Amazon.

Children's Works : Written and Illustrated under Pen Name, Kimmi.

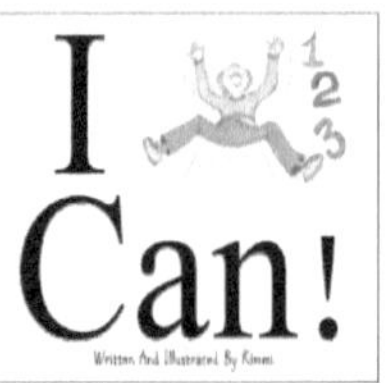

Contact:

Visit our website at alexmclellanbooks.com

Email: alexmclellanbooks@gmail.com

Twitter: @AKMcLellanBooks

MORE COMING SOON!

The Memoirs Of Mrs. Olivia Foxworthy & Always Olivia 2nd Editions

Carleah In Your Dreams, Vampiress 2nd Edition